Pumpkin Patch Sweethearts

Pumpkin Patch Sweethearts

A Welsh Sisters Romance

Sasha Summers

TULE
PUBLISHING

Dedication

Dedicated to Brenda Chin-for making my stories their best!

Dear Readers,

Welcome back to Crossvine Creek. The temperature is getting cooler, pumpkin spice is in the air, and it's time for Harley Welsh to fall in love. Just like *Dog Park Sweethearts*, this story is all about family, community, and love. The McBride family is new to town, but Harley is determined to make them feel right at home. And if she gets a little dreamy-eyed over Coach McBride, the handsome single father, all the better. So cuddle up with a warm blanket, some apple cider, and enjoy this sweet romance complete with the pumpkin carving, fall festival fun, a dog named Chewie, and two adorable kids who have found the woman they want to be their mother: Harley Welsh.

If you'd like to visit Crossvine Creek again, you are in luck. December 2020, a sweet Christmas Anthology, *Christmas Actually*, will features eleven holiday short stories by eleven fabulous authors. I'm thrilled to be part of this and hope you enjoy your return trip to Crossvine Creek!

Happy Reading!
Until the next book ~ Sasha Summers

Chapter One

"GOOD MORNING." HARLEY waved at Mr. Krieger and stepped aside, holding open the door of Corner Brew and Bakery. Cobie, her sister's large black Lab, sat patiently at her side. "How are you this morning, Mr. Krieger? Don't you just love the crisp fall air?"

"Makes my joints ache," Mr. Krieger answered, his mouth set in an ever-present downward slant.

"Sorry to hear that." Harley followed him inside, shortening the length of Cobie's leash. "We're all looking forward to coming to the farm to choose our pumpkins this year."

He made a garbled sound that might have been an 'I bet' though she wasn't one hundred percent certain. But there was no misunderstanding the way Mr. Krieger eyed her sister's dog with disapproval.

Harley knew Autumn's dog had better manners than most people, but Harley wasn't willing to take a chance—not after the look Mr. Krieger had shot their way. "Be a good girl, Cobie."

Cobie's ears perked up and her tail wagged, those big golden-brown eyes meeting Harley's.

"I know, I know. You're always a good girl," Harley added, feeling a need to apologize. She patted the dog on the head. Besides, Mr. Krieger was *always* grumpy.

"Harley," Georgia Lane called from her place behind the whitewashed counter. "What a nice surprise."

Normally, Autumn made their morning coffee run. Her sister was a morning person—spreading happiness wherever she went. "Autumn was running behind so I'm on coffee detail this morning." She smiled down at the dog. "Cobie offered to come with me, of course."

"It's nice to see you." Georgia smiled back. "You and Cobie are all bundled up. Is it that cold out there?"

"The wind has a bite to it." Harley glanced down at Cobie and grinned at the sweet black Lab. Autumn's beau, though, had the cutest little sweater-wearing dog in all of Crossvine Creek, Texas. She was pretty sure the only reason Cobie was wearing a sweater was so she and Baxter could match. Because that was the way Harley's sister thought.

"I don't know what smells better—the coffee or whatever it is that you're baking." Harley crossed the wide plank floor to the bakery case. The scent of freshly roasted coffee beans, pumpkin scones, and a hint of maple had Harley's stomach groaning, loudly.

Georgia's brows rose high. "Was that your stomach, child? You sound like you haven't eaten in a month."

"Maybe it's just how delicious everything smells," Harley countered, peering into the illuminated bakery case. Cupcake towers were stacked high with freshly glazed donuts, cinnamon rolls, and bear claws. Platters full of sugar crystal-dusted pumpkin muffins, cream cheese-frosted pumpkin scones, and maple and apple fritters were packed tight. "I was just going to get coffee for me and Autumn but now…"

"Not with your stomach growling like that, you're not," Georgia argued. "Arnie, make up a box of treats for Harley to take to the studio this morning. Make it a big box in case Noah stops by later—that boy can eat."

"Thank you." Harley smiled at Arnie Lane, Georgia's husband and co-owner of the busiest shop on Main Street. "I'm sure Noah will appreciate it." Her sister's boyfriend *did* stop by the art studio she and her sister owned most mornings.

"I'll get you set up." Arnie started assembling a cardboard pastry box.

"You want two coffees? Black?" Georgia asked.

"On a morning like this, I'm tempted to be extra daring. Two pumpkin lattes, please. With whipped cream." *Might as well go all in.* She tucked a strand of her long dark blond hair behind her ear and pulled her slim leather billfold from her matching Kate Spade purse. The duo was one of the few things she'd held on to from her New York days. For the most part, she'd been happy to leave any and all reminders of that time behind.

But this billfold had been the first thing she'd purchased after Global International Bank had commissioned a statue for their impressive all-glass foyer. It had been a turning point in her sculpture career. At least, that's what she'd thought at the time. With Grant, her childhood friend and another Crossvine Creek transplant, she'd explored the Big Apple and spent way too much money on her Kate Spade duo. She'd been so happy that day—but that had been before her big-city adventure had lost its sparkle.

Let it go. New York. Being a professional sculptor. Her doomed relationship with Oliver. That was a lifetime ago. One she didn't miss.

"All set?" Arnie asked.

"I think so." With her pastry box in a bag and her coffees in a drink carrier, she paid and tucked her wallet away, then thanked the Lanes and headed toward the door—moving quickly to step aside when the door swung open. Only she sidestepped, she tripped over Cobie's leash and—teetering on her heels—fell forward just enough to lose her drink carrier. Or rather, to launch the drink carrier into the air before making direct impact with the chest of the man who'd pushed the door open.

"I am so sorry," she gasped, staring at the man in horror—while Cobie began cleanup duty, wrapping her leash around Harley's legs. Harley looked up into the man's red, scowling face. "Oh. Oh no. I'm *so* sorry. Really." She took the napkins Arnie was offering and began blotting the man's broad chest—and his chin too. The guy was dripping. Hair, eyelashes, nose, chin… His shirt was damp and sticky beneath her hands. "I am truly sorry."

The man took a napkin from Arnie and wiped off his face, his bright blue eyes narrowing and his jaw muscle clenched tight. Even dripping coffee, this man looked good. Really, *really* good.

"She must have walked around when I was ordering." Harley kept blotting with one hand while trying to disentangle herself from Cobie and the leash with the other. Cobie, of course, was too busy lapping up the cream on the floor to pay much attention to her efforts. "Cobie," she urged, her anxiety growing the longer the man glared at her. His size, redness, and explosive sigh gave off a volcano soon-to-erupt vibe. Cobie looked up at her and sat, pulling the leash just tight enough to send Harley teetering forward again.

The man steadied her…right about the time a large dollop of whipped cream fell from his hair and landed on the tip of his nose—cinnamon and sugar crystals catching the light. And, much to her absolute mortification, she found herself giggling. With the man's glare, the helicopter sound of Cobie's nose searching the wood plank floor, and her mounting nerves…she just couldn't stop giggling. But she tried. She cleared her throat. "Really…I'm so…so sorry." She swallowed, but another giggle escaped.

The man swiped the cream from his nose, put the wadded napkins in the paper bag Arnie was holding out, and slid some bills across the counter.

"Oh no, please let me," Harley offered, finally leading

Cobie in a circle and untangling the leash. "It's the least I can do."

"I've got it." The man's voice was low and gruff and dripping impatience.

"Here you go." Arnie handed over three donut boxes stacked high and a cup of coffee. "See you later."

The man tilted his head toward Arnie, shot her a final disgusted look, then headed across the floor and out the bakery door.

Harley drew in a wavering breath. "Well, that's one way to start a Monday," she murmured. "I feel terrible."

"It's just a little coffee, Harley." Georgia waved her fears aside, chuckling. "No worries."

"Does he come often?" She stared after the man, his long stride carrying him down the sidewalk and away from the shop.

Arnie nodded. "Every Monday."

"Oh good." She slid her credit card across the counter. "Can you charge me for the next three Mondays please? I *do* feel really bad about the coffee—and the laughing."

Arnie shook his head, smiling. "You sure?"

"I'm sure." She glanced at the floor. "Cobie cleaned pretty thoroughly but the floor's probably going to be sticky." She frowned. "I can—"

"I'll mop it up, Harley, don't you worry," Arnie said. "Don't you let this ruin your morning. Especially on a Monday. You hear?"

"I do. You're right. I'll try." It would be easier if the man had accepted her apology—or had stopped glaring at her. He had to know it was all an unfortunate accident. She took her bag, two new coffees, and waved her good-byes.

By the time she'd made the walk from the bakery to Welsh Studios, she was second-guessing her decision to pay for his Monday indulgences. Maybe she should do something more immediate, to show how terrible she really felt? Because she did.

"Why are you frowning?" her sister, Autumn, asked as Harley closed the door behind her. "And why do you have a huge pastry box?"

"Georgia figured Noah might be stopping by later on," Harley said, sliding the box onto the counter.

"She is the sweetest." Autumn opened the box. "Oh, yum."

"That's what I thought, too." Harley picked up a maple-glazed croissant.

"And the frowning?" Autumn selected a pumpkin scone and closed the baker's box lid. "I know you're not a morning person but you're usually not quite this grumpy."

"This is the second round of pumpkin lattes... Because I doused a perfect stranger with the first batch," Harley admitted, her nose wrinkling. "Like, I soaked his shirt and laughed when I saw whipped cream hanging off his nose. And he was *so* angry. Red-faced, ready-to-blow angry."

"You bought us pumpkin lattes?" Autumn asked, opening her to-go coffee cup. "I'm so excited."

Harley smiled, shaking her head. "Autumn…"

"Did you intentionally throw the lattes on him?" Autumn asked, sipping her coffee.

"No." She sighed. "I sort of tripped over Cobie and—"

"It was an accident?" She waited for Harley's nod. "And, knowing you, you apologized?"

"Several times, but—"

"And he was still *angry* with you? Irritated, sure. But, come on, it was an accident," Autumn said, on the verge of frowning herself.

"Yes, he was… But then again, I did giggle—a lot—when the whipped cream splattered on his nose." She wrinkled her nose. "I couldn't seem to stop."

"Oh." Autumn shook her head, taking a sip of her latte. "Still, it's not like he was the victim of some aggressive latte-drenching. Is aggressive latte-drenching a crime?" She paused, shrugged, and kept going. "So what if he has to walk around smelling this good all day? I'm pretty sure this smells better than most aftershave and cologne. And it's seasonal—so he's being festive. He'll get over it and, probably wind up delighted he smells so yummy."

Only Autumn would come up with a scenario where the man would be grateful for what had happened. That was why she adored her big sister so much. She was, and always had been, one of a kind. "I don't think aggressive latte-drenching is a thing." Harley sipped her coffee. "If it is, I'm confident it's not a crime."

Autumn rolled her eyes. "Cobie, was there a mean man picking on your auntie Harley?"

Cobie sat, her tail wagging.

"Was he horribly mean and ugly?" Autumn asked.

Cobie's tail wagged faster.

"He wasn't ugly." Harley sighed, slipping her apron on. Before he'd had whipped cream on his nose, she'd noticed just how deep blue his eyes were... If he hadn't been glaring at her, she'd might have marveled over the spectrum of blue in his gaze. After all, she was an artist. Color was something she noticed. And the depth of blue in his eyes had been impressive. "And he wasn't mean. In fact, I don't think he said five words. He was just...irritated over the unintentional latte-drenching." She sipped her coffee, noticing her sister's curious expression. "What?"

"Nothing," Autumn said, nibbling at her scone. "So, who was this not ugly, irritated man you made smell delicious?"

"I don't know." Harley shrugged. "And since he's not here and we have a school bus arriving in, oh, fifteen minutes, I need to let it go. Besides, I told Arnie to charge me for his Monday order for the rest of the month. I mean, I do feel bad."

"Oh? So, he's a regular at the bakery?" Autumn asked. "That's very nice of you. I'm sure he'll appreciate it and forgive you for this rather unfortunate latte incident."

9

Harley went from desk to desk to lay out today's project supplies. There'd be no more worrying over pumpkin-latte man. Right this moment, there wasn't a thing she could do. Hopefully, the niggling guilt would ease over the course of the morning. But, guilty or not, the image of that dollop of whipped cream hanging off the man's nose still managed to make her smile.

THE FIRST WORDS out of his assistant coach's mouth were, "What's that smell?"

Josh didn't bother looking up from his notes. "Me." Lucky for him, he had a bunch of Crossvine Creek High School Football shirts to choose from. But there was nothing he could do about his splattered khakis.

"Any left?" Bernie asked, eyeing the donuts Josh had picked up earlier that morning.

Josh pushed the box across the top of his metal-topped desk. "There might be one."

"Thanks." Bernie Ulrich opened the box.

Considering his assistant coach's health, one was more than he needed. Josh was thankful the school nurse had told him about Bernie's previous heart attack and his high blood pressure—now he knew to keep an eye on his coworker.

Since Josh had accepted the head football coach position here at Crossvine Creek High School, he'd begun the slow process of getting to know the close-knit community. He was an outsider—meaning folk were kind, but wary. It would take time to make real friends and convince everyone he was here for the long haul.

"The team looks good. Strong. Ready for this weekend," Bernie said, sitting in the chair across from the desk, donut in hand. "If I were a betting man, I'd say our odds for Friday night's game look pretty good."

Josh placed his clipboard on the desk and sat back, running a hand along the back of his neck. "They do." The Crossvine Creek Wild Cats should win Friday—not that he'd jinx their chances by saying so out loud. Josh had come from a college campus, so he hadn't had much in the way of expectations. But the young men who made up the varsity football team had been a pleasant surprise. They had the drive to win, putting in the long hours they needed to hone their skills and strengthen their team as a whole.

"You're in for a treat. This is a grudge match—the Crossvine Creek Wild Cats versus the River Bend Bobcats. The whole town will turn out for this one. You'll see," Bernie added, finishing off his donut and glancing at the clock on his wall. "You headed out soon?"

Josh glanced at the clock, instantly panicking. "Yeah." He stood. "I should have left already."

Bernie winked. "You go on. I'll close up shop."

"You sure?" He grabbed his duffel bag, the pumpkin-scented shirt inside perforating the canvas fabric. *Great.*

"I'm sure." Bernie waved. "You tell little Nadia I said hello."

Josh smiled. "Will do."

It didn't take long to reach his house—nothing was too far apart in Crossvine Creek. He left the high school, headed down Main Street, took a left on Maple Lane, and a right on Ash Drive. His house, 431 Ash Drive, sat smack in the middle of the block. When he pulled into the driveway of his craftsman cottage, he braced himself. Next door, rocking away in her wicker rocking chair, was Bev Washington. She was a nice lady but she tended to be a little *overly* neighborly—full of questions and curiosity about him and his family.

"Evening, Coach," she called as soon as he opened the door on his Jeep. "How'd practice go? We sure are excited about the game this Friday."

"Me too, Mrs. Washington," he said, heading around to the front porch.

"You go on and call me Bev, Coach." She waved. "Give your little miss a smile for me."

"Will do." Josh waved back, his step quickening as he ran up the porch steps, opened the front door, then quickly shut it behind him, breathing a sigh of relief. "I'm home," he called out, grinning at the rapid footsteps coming down the stairs and straight for him. "Hey, darlin'." He held his arms wide, scooping up his daughter and hugging her close. "How're you this evening?"

Nadia wrapped her arms around his neck. "Good." She

sniffed. "You smell funny, Daddy."

"Don't I know it." He kissed her cheek. "Some lady poured her coffee all over me."

Nadia's eyes went round. "Why?"

He shrugged. "She was all tangled up in her dog's leash and fell over." Good thing he'd steadied her. As twisted up as she was, she could have taken a hard fall. Not that she'd have noticed. She'd been too busy laughing at him.

"Poor lady." Nadia patted him. "Poor Daddy."

"Poor Daddy, is right." He carried her down the hall and into the family room.

"Evening, Coach McBride," Bertha Reed said, as she stirred a pot on the stove. "I made a pot of chili and there's some corn bread muffins in the oven. Also, little Nadia has a reminder note from her teacher about her art show tomorrow night."

"Thank you, Mrs. Reed." Josh didn't know what he'd do without the woman. She'd retired from the high school just last year and had been looking for part-time work about the same time he and his family had moved to town. Not only did she pick up Nadia from kindergarten, she made dinner, and offered to grocery shop now and then. "I've got it on the calendar and programmed it into my phone. I wouldn't miss it." Since they'd moved, art was about the only thing Nadia was interested in. According to her teacher, his little girl was awkward and shy at school—making it hard for his five-year-old daughter to make friends in their new hometown.

"I figured." Mrs. Reed smiled. "Well now. I'll head home to my Fred, then."

"Night, Mrs. Reed," he said.

"Night, Mrs. Reed," Nadia said, waving.

"Night, sweet girl." Mrs. Reed hung the apron she'd been wearing on the side of the refrigerator. "Night, Tucker. Sorry I wasn't more help with your homework. Now, if it was history, we'd be fine."

"Thanks anyway, Mrs. Reed. I appreciate the offer." His ten-year-old son, Tucker, had homework spread out on the kitchen table.

With another nod and wave, Mrs. Reed left.

"How's it going?" Josh asked his son.

"This experimental method thing makes my head hurt." Tucker tapped his pencil eraser against the stack of papers.

He ruffled his son's hair. "You'll figure it out. You always do. But I'm happy to help, if you need it?"

"Thanks, Dad." Tucker sat back in the cane kitchen chair and stared up at him. "What's with the new cologne?"

"It's not cologne." He chuckled, setting Nadia in the chair beside her big brother. "It's coffee."

"A poor lady fell on Daddy and spilled her coffee on him," Nadia explained.

"Yup." Josh headed into the kitchen for a glass of water. "How about I take a shower, get these clothes in the washing machine, and then we'll eat some dinner?"

Nadia gave him a thumbs-up.

"We'll set the table," Tucker offered. "Won't we, Squirt?"

Nadia nodded.

"Sounds like a plan," he said, smiling. There were times he'd love to just stand still and look at them. Like now. Not too long—or they'd notice and worry. But long enough to ground him. "When I get back, I won't smell like—"

"A pumpkin pie?" Nadia asked.

He chuckled again and headed up the stairs to his room. After a shower, he dressed and carried his clothes into the laundry room. Mrs. Reed had washed, folded, and piled up the kids' clothes on the counter. He'd told her she didn't need to do that, but she'd waved his protests aside and promised she'd leave his clothes alone. Once Mrs. Reed had found out he was a widower, she'd given him a look of motherly sympathy. He'd tried to assure her he'd been taking care of things for four years now but she wasn't listening.

In retrospect, he appreciated the extra work she did. Most nights, he came home so tired, he was in no shape to cook, let alone make sure the kids' clothes were clean and folded. Things would slow down when football season was over. But, for now, it was early mornings and long afternoon practices. He didn't know what he'd do without Mrs. Reed.

He turned on the washing machine, added soap, and tossed his dirty clothes inside. The pumpkin smell was downright overpowering.

All day long, he'd been reminded of the woman he'd been so rude to. It had been an accident. He knew that. The look of horror and surprise on her face reflected all the things he was feeling—plus the sting of hot coffee. She'd apologized over and over and what had he done? Nothing. Well, something. He'd snapped at her.

Could he blame her for laughing? The whole whipped cream thing had been kind of funny. He should have laughed. But he'd always had a hard time laughing at himself…

His mood had nothing to do with the coffee and everything to do with how rough his morning had already been up to that point. Nadia had been crying when he'd dropped her off at kindergarten, begging him to stay with her, or asking to go back home—to their real home. He'd reminded her that this was home now—it had been for five months. Since they'd moved over the summer, Josh had hoped Nadia would settle in once the school year had started. Instead, she'd become clingier than ever. He'd been tempted to keep her with him. Unwinding her little arms from his neck had ripped at his heart. Even after he'd left, after he'd driven to the bakery, he'd still felt her arms around him and heard her sobs in his ears. And then—well, then he'd been wearing coffee and holding on to a stranger.

A stranger with light brown eyes, curly hair, rosy cheeks, and a husky laugh that had caught his full attention. Maybe that's why he hadn't laughed. It'd been so long since he'd felt even a hint of interest in a woman, he'd been rattled. And, pumpkin latte scent aside, he couldn't deny there was a *hint* of interest.

Chapter Two

"That is the prettiest little bird I have ever seen." Harley knelt beside the table, watching the little girl use her thumbs to smooth out the clay with intense focus. "Beautiful feathers."

Nadia smiled at her. "It's a dove," she whispered.

"Does your dove have a name?" Harley whispered back.

"Lolly," Nadia whispered.

"I like that." Harley beamed. "I bet Lolly sings the prettiest songs."

Nadia nodded, looking proud and sweet and shy all at the same time.

Since the school district had suffered budget cuts, art had been one of the first programs to go. Through donors and grants, Harley and Autumn had worked hard to make sure that the children of Crossvine Creek had access to the studio. Her hometown was small but art had always been a big part of it. Taking the chance to learn about art away from future generations had seemed just plain wrong—at least to the Welsh family.

Accommodating classrooms of thirty or more students

wasn't easy but it was worth it to Harley and her sister. And when they had a gifted student like Nadia, it was pure joy. The moment she'd walked into the studio, Harley had felt an instant connection with the little girl. Like Nadia, Harley had been a painfully shy child. If not for her big sister Autumn, Harley would have stayed home reading or in the family studio all the time. But, as far as Harley could tell, Nadia didn't have a big sister to help bring her—or drag her—out of her shell.

"Would you like to put Lolly with your other work?" Harley asked, pointing at the tabletop where the little girl's artwork had been arranged for tonight's art showcase.

Nadia shrugged. "Not finished."

"That's okay." Harley sat on the child-sized chair at the little girl's side. "It will show your family what you're working on next. It doesn't have to be finished to be beautiful."

Nadia's big blue eyes studied the bird for a long time before she said, "Okay."

"We can work on it some more on Thursday," Harley offered. "What does Lolly need to be finished?"

Nadia carried the bird to the table with her name neatly printed. "She needs blue paint. Blue was my Lolly's favorite color. She wore blue every day." She sat the bird down with extra care.

"Like your eyes?" Harley asked. Lolly was named after someone special. Who was she and would she be there tonight to cheer on Nadia's creative efforts? "By the time you come on Thursday, Lolly will be dry and ready for her blue paint."

Nadia smiled, holding up her clay-smeared hands. "Wash-up time?"

"Good idea." As much as Harley wanted to be Nadia's personal helper, she knew there was a room full of students getting ready to depart. Preparing for the arrival of a large class was one thing. Cleanup? Well, it would take her and Autumn the full four hours before the Art Showcase this evening to make the studios presentable.

Once the bus was loaded and the studio was empty, Harley returned to the little bird on Nadia's table.

"You're really smitten with her, aren't you?" Autumn asked, sliding an arm around Harley's waist. "She's your mini-me, you know that, don't you? So shy it hurts. And bursting with talent."

Harley slid her arm around her sister's waist. "I do. Her teacher, Miss Reyes, says Nadia's having a hard time settling in."

"Poor thing. I can only imagine how hard a move would be at her age. Any move, period. I mean, we've spent our whole lives here." Autumn gave her a squeeze and let go. "Are Nadia's parents coming tonight?"

Harley began collecting the clay remnants for later use. "I hope so." She pressed the airtight lid on the container and returned the large bin to the shelf.

"Where's the tornado?" Noah Contreras asked, assessing the classroom from the doorway.

"Tornado Kindergarten is probably back at the elementary school by now." Autumn crossed the room, turning her face up for a kiss from her sweetie. "Hi."

"Hi." Noah was all too willing to give her a kiss.

Harley smiled and turned back to the cleanup. The two of them, together, radiated a whole crazy-in-love vibe. Harley's one attempt at love had failed so epically, she wasn't sure she'd ever have a they-lived-happily-ever sort of relationship. She'd put it all out there, invested her whole heart, but it hadn't been enough for Oliver. Correction, *she* hadn't been enough for Oliver. Not as she was. To him, she'd been a work in progress—a partner he could mold and shape into his ideal woman.

It all worked out for the best.

She'd thought venturing to New York on her own had taken courage. But standing up for herself and returning Oliver's massive diamond ring had been the greater test. What if he was right? What if his list of 'areas of improvement' was his way of helping her become the best version of herself? What if wanting to pursue art after they were married had been selfish? And maybe it wouldn't have been so bad to wait to have kids until he'd secured a partnership at his law firm... He'd made it all sound so logical. Practical. It had taken weeks for her to realize the truth. Oliver didn't love her—not the way a man should love the woman he wanted to marry. Real love, the love her parents had shared, was unconditional. And she would never, ever, marry a man who didn't love her for who she was.

Autumn had that.

Her father's relationship with Cynthia seemed to be heading that way.

Someday, maybe, she'd find the man for her. If not— well, she was happy. It might have taken her a while to figure it all out, but she had. Now, she was doing exactly what she wanted to do, in a place she loved.

"I'll mop," Noah offered.

"You're a prince." Harley started collecting paintbrushes while Autumn began the tedious task of scraping all the bits of glue and paint and dried clay from the table and countertops. Once the paintbrushes were washed and hung on the drying rack, Harley went to help Autumn, following up with a thorough disinfection.

"Way better," Noah said, rolling the wheeled mop and bucket from the room. "I brought burgers from Burger Barn. Shakes too. I put those in the freezer."

"What a man." Autumn stood on tiptoes to give Noah another kiss.

Harley headed into the lobby and their waiting burgers. Baxter, Noah's adorable little sweater-wearing dog, and Cobie sat at the ready, tails wagging and ears perked up. "Oh, I know it smells good. But I'm starving, so you're just going to have to wait until your parents feed you."

She ate, then hurried into the bathroom to change. Exhibitions were a big deal, no matter how old the artists. So it was important to shed her studio-ready clothes and dress up—as special occasions required. She tugged on her form-fitting black turtleneck sweater dress, her high-heel black boots, tugged her hair into a slick knot at the back of her head, and dabbed on some red-tinted lip gloss. She wore a mosaic cross she'd made, some gold bangle hoops, and shrugged. *Fancy but not* too *fancy.*

At seven o'clock, the families started arriving.

She understood the thrill of accomplishment that came with completing a piece of art. But for these children, it was twofold. They felt accomplishment for themselves *and* approval, through their parents' presence and involvement.

When the clock read eight, Harley worried Nadia and her family wouldn't show—until a little hand tugged on her skirt. "Nadia." She knelt, smiling at the little girl. "You look so pretty tonight."

Nadia's black long-sleeve dress was covered in tiny pumpkins and leaves. Her words were the softest of whispers, "Miss Harley." She leaned in close and added, "We match."

"We do. My dress doesn't have pumpkins though. I like yours better." She resisted the urge to hug the little girl. She wanted to, she did. But Nadia was so shy—she didn't want to scare the little girl off. "Who did you bring with you?" she asked, looking up. "Oh." The man. *The* mountain of a man. The one she'd fallen into, doused with coffee, and then laughed at… The man with those blue-blue eyes. It was him, all right. From Corner Brew and Bakery. She stood slowly, beyond surprised. "Well…"

"Pumpkin latte," the man said. As his gaze swept over her, she saw the slightest tick of his jaw muscle.

"Most people know me as Harley Welsh." She cleared her throat and offered him her hand. "Miss Welsh. Or Miss Harley."

His hand engulfed hers. Warm. Strong. Rough. "Josh McBride, Nadia's father. Or Coach McBride, over at the high school."

"Oh." *This* man was Nadia's father? He was so…so…athletic and…gruff… And big. Not at all the way she'd envisioned Nadia's father would be. Or a father in general. *What does that even mean?*

"Tucker." Nadia spoke so softly Harley had to crouch at the little girl's side again to hear her. "This is my brother."

"It's nice to meet you, Tucker." Harley smiled at the boy standing beside Nadia. "I see a definite resemblance." All three of them had brilliant blue eyes and dark brown hair. Where Nadia's face was still round and childlike, Tucker's was slimming down, with shades of his father's strong jaw and the slight cleft in his chin evident. Tucker and Nadia both had great smiles. Josh McBride? Well, since he hadn't and wasn't smiling, that had yet to be determined. "I don't think I've had you for class yet, Tucker?"

"Next semester." Tucker was taking it all in. "This is

cool."

"Thanks. My sister and I try to keep it that way." Josh McBride might not be smiling at her but he didn't seem to have a problem looking at her. More like openly assessing. Apparently, he was rude, even when he wasn't wearing coffee. *With whipped cream hanging off his nose.* She had to smile at the mental image. Instead of worrying over his silent, judge-y-ness, she focused all of her attention on Nadia. Nadia, who was sort of peering around her brother, her gaze bouncing around the room at her classmates, looking more and more disconcerted. Harley asked, "Have you shown them your art, yet?"

Nadia shook her head.

"Show us, Squirt. You were all excited on the way here." Tucker was restless, all youthful energy.

Nadia frowned at her brother but didn't say anything.

The little girl was shy and, now, embarrassed. Poor little thing was so out of her element. "I'm glad you were excited. You should be," Harley encouraged. "They are going to be so surprised to see what you've made."

"She's always talking about Miss Harley." Tucker tugged on his little sister's hand, earning him a smile. "Miss Harley this and Miss Harley that—"

"I'll tell you a secret." Harley leaned forward, and whispered. "I always look forward to when your class is coming to the studio. You can ask Miss Autumn. I talk about you a lot too."

Nadia's grin was wide and bright as she reached up and took Harley's hand. "Let's show them."

"Let's." Harley let Nadia lead the way.

Nadia stopped in front of the small white-topped table displaying her work. "This."

"Wow, Squirt." Tucker was wide-eyed as he assessed his little sister's art. "Seriously?"

"Seriously," Harley said. "This is *all* her. No help from anyone."

"You get me more clay," Nadia argued. "And paint. And help me wash my hands."

"Well, I do that much." Harley nodded, stepping aside so Josh McBride could get a better view of his daughter's handiwork. "But helping with supplies isn't the same thing as making art." She risked a glance his way.

Josh McBride was studying Nadia's flower bud vase, her pinch pot, the simple mosaic coaster, and her beautiful little bird. "This is beautiful, Nadia." He pulled up one of the kid-size chairs and sat, drawing his daughter close. "Tell me about this one." He pointed at the coaster.

"It's a pattern," Nadia said, running her little pointer finger over the beads. "I pressed them in. Miss Harley said this is a…a…fading rainbow." She looked up at Harley.

"All her design." Harley'd marveled at Nadia's concentration. Bead by bead, she'd managed to arrange her circular pattern in a color wheel, from the lightest shade to the darkest.

Josh smiled at his daughter, pressing a kiss against her temple. "I'm impressed."

"Daddy." Nadia blushed, staring up at the man with open adoration.

Harley's heart thumped. Not just because this giant man was sitting in a kid-sized chair giving his daughter affection but because it was clear, to Nadia, this man hung the moon. Maybe he wasn't as bad as he came across. Maybe, like Nadia, he wasn't good with people. But he was a coach… So maybe he wasn't good with adults?

"Miss Harley says I'm good at art," Nadia said.

"Miss Harley is right." Josh McBride turned those blue eyes her way.

"I normally am." Harley shrugged. "When it comes to art, anyway." She hadn't quite been prepared for the devastating effect his quick laugh would have on her. Or his smile. Devastating in that she felt inordinately warm and oddly breathless at the velvet-rich timbre of his voice.

"How do you do that?" Tucker asked, pointing at the pots her more advanced students had created. "They're all shiny."

"A kiln," Harley said. "Nadia, do you want to show him?"

"But we can't touch it." Nadia took her brother's hand. "It gets real hot."

"No touching. Got it, Squirt." Tucker stooped to listen to her as they walked to the back of the classroom.

Josh stood, content to inspect his daughter's projects. "Did she really do this on her own?"

"Cross my heart, it's all Nadia. Your daughter is talented." Harley nodded. "And focused—especially for a five-year-old."

He faced her. "Is focused another way of telling me she doesn't talk much?"

Harley shook her head. "She talks to me. But with her classmates, she's shy."

"Very." One eyebrow rose. "But when she does talk, it's about being here. This," he said, pointing at Nadia's sculptures. "And you."

The man was intense. *Intense*, intense. She ran a hand over her hair, smoothing any escaping curls and steadying her hands. "Like I said, she's...she's special." She smiled. "The first day of class we gave them each a mound of clay to explore. Most kids made a pile of balls or carved letters or smiley faces into it. And that's fine—it's just so they get the feel for the weight and texture. But Nadia didn't do that." She paused, watching him. "She stared at it. The whole time, she sat there, I could tell she was contemplating all her ideas, not sure where to start."

He continued to stare at her—silent—his expression as blank as ever.

"I was like her, you see. Shy and awkward but full of creativity." She cleared her throat. "Which brings me around to something I'd like to discuss with you."

The brow rose again, his arms crossed, but he remained silent.

"I think Nadia would enjoy private lessons." She swallowed, acutely aware of the slow downward tilt of his mouth. "She's—"

"Talented." He sighed. "So talented she needs private lessons?"

"Well…yes." His tone got her back up. "If you're agreeable—"

"To pay for art lessons?" he asked, running a hand along the back of his neck. "You think private lessons are necessary? For a five-year-old?"

Harley blinked, processing his words and the slight downward twist of his mouth. Coach McBride wasn't an art fan, then. Or was it something else? A nasty suspicion took root. Wait… Did he really think she'd been buttering him up for…for a sale? Didn't he see how Nadia was struggling? Or how the little girl lit up when she was here? Harley couldn't decide whether she was angry or offended. Either way, she wasn't happy.

She took a deep breath and tried her best to remain professional. "Mr. McBride, you don't know me and I don't know you, so I suppose there might be some confusion about my motivation. It was Miss Reyes, Nadia's teacher, who suggested the lessons. According to *her*, Nadia engages here. She thought it would help Nadia settle in and express herself—normalize her new environment." She swallowed against the tightening of her throat. *I'm not trying to take advantage of your precious little girl—a little girl who is struggling to make friends.* But all she said was, "You should speak with Miss Reyes." By the time she'd finished, she was shaking all over again—even her voice trembled. *So much for professionalism.*

But she didn't have time to be out of sorts because Nadia was dragging her brother back, all smiles, and Harley wasn't about to let anything steal that happiness away tonight.

JOSH HAD KNOWN Miss Welsh was important to his daughter—just not how much. But the instant they'd walked inside Welsh Studios, Nadia had lit up. She'd only let go of his hand when she'd lasered in on the woman. Once Nadia had tugged him closer, she'd hung on Harley Welsh's every word and glowed from the woman's praise. He didn't know what he'd expected, but this wasn't it. A quick scan of Nadia's classmates' tables removed any doubts that Nadia's skill level was above average. His little girl wasn't just playing with Play-Doh and finger paint, she was creating art.

Which is what Miss Welsh had been trying to tell him...

Miss Welsh. *She* had been the last person he'd expected to see here tonight. *She* was Nadia's art teacher? *She* was the one showering his little girl with sincere praise and encouragement? Once again, the woman—Harley Welsh—had rattled him.

He sighed.

When Miss Reyes was done directing her other students and their families around the studio, he'd speak with her. It bothered him that Nadia's teacher would discuss his daughter with Miss Welsh before she'd mentioned anything to him. Nadia was *his* daughter. He was the one who needed to be having these discussions with Nadia's teacher. The *only* one.

He was doing his best here. But no matter how hard he tried, he couldn't shake the feeling that something was missing. Worse, he didn't know what it was or how to fix it. His kids were everything to him. *Everything.* They'd all had a rough year and it would take time for them to settle into their new routine, but he was willing to do whatever it took to make that happen.

As much as he'd like to think art would help Nadia, it seemed too easy. Miss Welsh's well-meaning suggestion was just that—well-meaning. She didn't know a thing about what he and his children had been through the last year.

But...Harley Welsh *did* seem to understand his Nadia. And Nadia...well, Nadia adored her Miss Harley.

"This place is pretty cool," Tucker said. "I always thought art was sort of...nerdy." He shrugged.

"Is that a bad thing?" Harley Welsh laughed, far more at ease now that his kids were there. "My sister and I have always sort of embraced the whole art-nerd thing. My father was an artist. He taught us to be true to ourselves, no matter what the rest of the world thought."

"You? You're not a nerd." Tucker gave Harley a quick look, his cheeks flushing and his smile more awkward than normal. "At all."

Josh had a pretty good idea what his son was thinking. Namely, Harley Welsh was pretty. Really pretty. Especially when she was smiling. With her fancy hairstyle, form-fitting dress, and high-heeled black boots, nerd was the last word he'd associate with Harley Welsh. Classy. Elegant. *Beautiful.* And maybe a little clumsy… He'd washed his gym bag four times and still the unmistakable scent of pumpkin lingered.

"Nadia, did you show them what you're working on right now?" Harley asked, her gaze darting his way, then moving back to his daughter. "It might be my favorite yet. Her bird."

Nadia's blue gaze dropped to the wide wood-planked studio floor as she said, "I named it Lolly. Lolly-bird."

He did his best not to react. Lolly was their grandmother. His mother. He knew the kids missed her—he did, too. No one had had as much zest for life—her booming voice, off-key singing, and laughter had filled his childhood. She'd been gone eight months, but there were times he could still hear her chuckle. There was something about the delicate little bird, his daughter's tiny fingerprints pressed into the clay, that knocked the air from his lungs and pressed hard against his chest. "Lolly-bird, huh?" He cleared his throat.

Nadia's gaze met his. "She liked to sing."

"All the time." Tucker bent low to study the bird. "She liked birds, too."

Nadia joined her brother. "I'll paint it blue."

He saw the tightening of his son's jaw, heard the waver in his daughter's voice, and wound up kneeling to drape an arm around them both. "When it's all done, we'll find someplace special for your Lolly-bird. Sound good?"

Nadia nodded.

He ruffled Tucker's hair, hugged Nadia close, and stood—to find Harley Welsh watching them, wide-eyed with sympathy. When those light brown eyes locked with his, he realized his mistake. Harley Welsh *truly* cared about his little girl—it was written all over the woman's face. Considering how hard Nadia was taking the move and settling here in Crossvine Creek, his little girl needed all the love and support she could get. He'd let his pride get the best of him—again. His wife's battle with cancer had been quick—a mere eight months between her diagnosis and the day he lost her. He'd barely come to terms with her illness when she passed.

After her death, he'd struggled to keep it together—determined to fight against his grief and stay strong. Tucker had been five, Nadia a tiny baby, and he'd just lost the woman he loved. Thank God he'd had help. His mother had known what he was going through and hadn't let him shut her out. He wasn't sure which had been harder for Lolly:

teaching him humility or giving up her little cottage and moving in to help him with the kids. He was still working on the humility. His mother had done her best to teach him there was no shame in needing help—or taking it when it was offered—but it wasn't easy for him. If his mother had still been around, she'd likely put him in his place for being so rude to Harley Welsh. Miss Welsh, who was only trying to help.

"Mr. McBride." Nadia's teacher, Miss Reyes, chose that moment to approach. "I'm so glad you could come and see just how gifted your daughter is."

"I wouldn't miss it." He needed to add 'keeping the edge out of his voice' to the list of things he was working on. He tried again, speaking with care. "Nadia goes on and on about being here." He risked a glance Harley Welsh's way. "And Miss Harley."

"Oh, don't I know it." Miss Reyes smiled at his daughter. "If Nadia could spend every day, all day, with Miss Harley, I'm certain she would. And who would blame her? Everything about this place is welcoming and encouraging." Miss Reyes patted Nadia on the shoulder. "Miss Harley most of all. Right, Nadia?"

There it was again, pure adoration on his daughter's face as she stared up at her art teacher. Apparently, both his kids were entranced by the woman.

"Do you have a moment?" Miss Reyes asked.

"I was going to show Tucker and Nadia the new supplies

we got today in the back, if that's okay with you Mr. McBride? It won't take long." Harley Welsh probably already knew what Miss Reyes was about to say—likely something to do with art lessons.

"Sure." He watched Nadia eagerly take Harley Welsh's hand, still smiling. There was no sign of the hunched shoulders, shy gazes, or shuffling steps that had been so much a part of his Nadia lately. No, in that moment, she seemed just like a carefree five-year-old. The sight left an ache in his chest. "Miss Welsh mentioned something about art lessons?"

Miss Reyes nodded. "Did she? I'm glad. I know Nadia is young but, as you can see, she's quite relaxed here."

He saw.

"Miss Welsh and her sister have a long waiting list for new students but she's assured me she'd be happy to make room for Nadia. There would be a scholarship available for her too, if you're interested." Miss Reyes paused. "She and your daughter have, for lack of a better word, clicked."

A waiting list. A scholarship. He ran a hand along the back of his neck, zeroing in on Nadia's art. Harley Welsh was willing to make room for Nadia? For free? *Because Nadia is special to her.* That clinched it—he was *definitely* a jerk.

"Of course, it would have to fit with your schedule. I know coaching, especially at this time of the year, must keep you extra busy." Miss Reyes smiled. "And of course, there's the big rivalry game this weekend."

He was busy, but not too busy for his children. He didn't want to be that kind of father. A slower pace of life was one of the benefits of a town like Crossvine Creek, and it was the reason he'd moved in the first place. Yes, high school football was important in Texas, but Crossvine Creek had pretty low expectations. Had they offered him a surprisingly impressive compensation package to get their team whipped into a more competitive state? Yes. Was his continued employment contingent on the team's progress? Yes. But pre-employment negotiations had eased some of his reticence. They weren't expecting the team to win the state championship this year. Next year? That was a different story.

A lot could happen in a year. For now, he wanted to slow down, wanted to give his children time—without stressing over job security. Crossvine Creek was one of the few Texas towns that seemed to have the whole academics, sports, and the arts thing balanced out. And balance was what he and his children needed right now.

"So...her behavior is no different in class?" He held his breath, knowing the answer but hoping he was wrong.

Miss Reyes's smile faltered just a bit. "Well, as you know, mornings are rough. She does settle down but she's still having a hard time engaging with her classmates."

Which was exactly what he feared. Her shyness seemed to increase daily. There were times his little girl seemed to be fading into the background and it scared him. "I'll talk to

Miss Welsh." Considering how well that had gone the first time, he'd best start with an apology. "If you think more time here would help, then that's what we will do."

"I think that's a wonderful idea," Miss Reyes agreed. "Well, if you'll excuse me, another family has arrived and I should go greet them. Good luck with the game on Friday, Coach."

As she walked away, he pulled his phone from his pocket to take a few pictures of Nadia's art. Since Harley Welsh hadn't returned with his children, he made a slow circuit around the classroom. He was no pro but there was a clear difference between the students' art and that of the teachers. He wasn't sure which sister was responsible for the series of finely sculpted flowers and blown glass vases, but they were certainly impressive. It was the attention to detail that caught his eye. The veins on the leaf. The sense of movement to the stem. The wafer-thin petal with a slightly ruffled edge.

"I know," a woman said, pointing at the sculptures. "She's got some mad skills." She held her hand out. "I'm the other Welsh—Autumn. Harley is my sister. Which one is yours?" Her brown gaze swept over the dwindling crowd.

"Nadia."

"Nadia?" Autumn turned. "Oh, she is the cutest thing ever. She and Harley have some sort of mind-meld thing going on. I swear, you rewind time and Harley would have been Nadia's twin."

That was hard to believe but the thought had him smiling all the same.

"Where is Nadia?" Autumn asked, a crease between her brows.

"Miss Welsh took her to see something? In the back?" He shrugged. "I know you're wanting to wrap things up though, so I should probably locate them."

"Oh." Autumn smiled. "I bet I know where they are." She pointed. "If you go down the hall, the last door on the right, you should find them."

He thanked her and followed her directions. He paused in the doorway of what had to be a storeroom, wondering why Tucker and Nadia—a familiar large black Lab between them—were staring at the box at their feet.

"I know," Harley Welsh was saying. "I don't even know where to start. But I have to sort them out. People will want to buy a whole set."

"Wow." Tucker was shaking his head. "Just wow."

"Yep," Harley Welsh said.

Nadia stared up at her. "I can help."

"I would love your help, Nadia." Harley Welsh nodded. "But we should probably ask your dad first, don't you think?"

"Ask me what?" he asked, leaning against the door.

"Miss Harley's supplies exploded," Nadia said, pointing inside the box.

"She has to have a mouth, a nose, two eyes, and two ears boxed up to sell." Tucker frowned. "They're all mixed together."

Josh stepped closer, peering into the box. "Looks like a bunch of spare Mr. and Mrs. Potato Head pieces."

"You're right." Harley leaned forward. "That is exactly what it looks like."

The large black Lab turned, ears cocked up and tail wagging, to sniff his feet and circle him.

"I remember you," Josh said, staring down at the dog. "No leash, this time." His gaze drifted to Harley's.

"Isn't Cobie the coolest?" his son gushed. "When we get a dog, we should get one just as cool and smart as she is."

"Are you getting a dog?" Harley asked. "How exciting. Cobie is my sister's but I love getting to dog-sit. Autumn or I can help you find a great dog—we both volunteer at the animal shelter here in town."

"We're *talking* about getting a dog," Josh interrupted. The kids had been after him for a dog since they'd discovered the large dog park in the middle of Town Square Park. Every family walk seemed to wind up with them sitting on a park bench, watching the dogs and their owners having fun.

"I do want one," Nadia added, gently stroking Cobie's ear between her thumb and fingers. "Soft, like Cobie."

"I didn't say no. I just said a dog is a lot of work." He sighed, not ready to commit to more responsibility. Not yet. They were, all of them, still figuring things out.

"Your dad is right," Harley said. "A dog is a lot of work. And they need training. You wouldn't want your dog tripping someone or...making you spill your coffee on someone." Her light brown eyes met his. "Especially if it was pumpkin coffee."

His brows shot up, the urge to smile growing.

"I don't drink coffee," Tucker said, looking confused. "Or pumpkin coffee. Gross." Tucker's facial expression had Harley laughing.

Josh had to smile then—for a second or two. There it was again, that husky laugh that knocked around his insides. The longer his gaze was locked with Harley Welsh's, the tighter his throat felt. But he managed to say, "Agreed. The smell of pumpkin coffee is hard to wash out too." He wasn't sure what to make of this or—if he was being honest—how to feel about Harley Welsh or her laugh or her smile. He blew out a long, slow breath and stared into the box of plastic eyes and lips and ears, clearing his mind and running through what he did know.

Nadia adored her.

Miss Reyes trusted her.

Tucker was quickly developing a crush on her.

While all evidence indicated she was this wonderful, caring, beautiful woman... *Beautiful?* That had nothing to do with any of this. Bottom line? Nadia needed more than just her father and brother. That someone was clearly Harley Welsh. She was making room for his daughter, expecting no compensation, because she cared about Nadia.

He ran a hand along the back of his neck, knowing the

choice was made: Nadia would be taking art lessons. Since he'd be seeing a lot more of Harley Welsh, he'd have to get used to being rattled.

Chapter Three

"I'M PRETTY SURE he is the man Bev Washington was talking about," Autumn said, tucking the loose end of her mile-long leaf-embroidered scarf into the collar of her high-school letter jacket. "She said he was the high school coach, didn't she?"

"I don't remember." Harley tugged the belt of her black-and-white polka-dot coat tighter. Bev Washington seemed to have a new potential soul mate for Harley every time she ran into the woman—it was hard to keep them all straight.

"But he *was* the one you left smelling like a pumpkin latte, yes?" Autumn giggled. "Ooh, now I have a total mental picture of that."

"Yep. It wasn't pretty. I did apologize. Even though it was sort of funny..." Harley wrinkled her nose. "I don't think he's forgiven me, though. He mentioned it at the art show—how hard it was to get the pumpkin smell out." She shrugged. The whole run-in with Josh McBride had left her...disconcerted. Maybe it was because of the way he looked at her. Studying? Assessing? Judging? But she almost preferred that expression to his smile. His smile had been...

Well, a *lot*.

"Who are we talking about?" Noah asked, his arm hooked through Autumn's and the tip of his nose red. "And why is it cold? This is Texas."

"Exactly." Autumn smiled up at him. "Give it a half an hour and we'll need our sundresses. Well, you won't, of course, but...you know what I mean."

Noah was staring down at Autumn with pure affection. "I think I do."

"Coach McBride," Autumn said.

"What?" Noah asked, still recovering from the blinding smile Autumn had sent his way.

"We're talking about the hunky new coach who was checking Harley out during the student art show." Autumn didn't even bother to keep her voice down.

"Autumn," Harley growled, tugging her sister's arm. "That is *not* true. Besides, someone could hear you." Someone like Bev Washington or one of her book club friends. *Talk about worst-case scenario.* While she adored the troupe of elderly ladies, she wasn't crazy about their penchant for gossip or matchmaking. If they'd heard Autumn... Well, it would be bad for Harley. And since it was tradition for everyone in Crossvine Creek to go to the rivalry match between the Crossvine Creek Wild Cats and the River Bend Bobcats, chances were that the book club ladies were all here somewhere.

"See?" Autumn whispered, smiling at Noah.

"See, what?" Harley asked, noting the glance between them.

"I told Noah you might just be crushing on Coach McBride, too." Autumn shrugged.

"No. Autumn, no. That's a hard no. Not a maybe disguised as a no—just a no." Harley sighed, coming to a stop. "Now, Noah, I'd like you to hear it from me. That way you can remind my beloved sister of my sincere objections. I am *not* crushing on Coach McBride." She paused, staring at her sister. "Not in the least. He's made it clear he doesn't think all that highly of me, either." His implication that her praise for Nadia had been part of a sales pitch had stung. "In fact, I'm confident Coach McBride does not like me."

"You did pour your coffee all over me the first time we met." The voice was low and deep and all too familiar.

Harley froze. Even her heart seemed to skip a beat. *No, no, no.* How much had Coach McBride heard? She scowled at her sister, then turned. Luckily, Tucker and Nadia were standing next to him so she could pretend she hadn't said anything *that* embarrassing. Or at least, she could try. "Evening, McBride family." She risked a glance Josh McBride's way, hoping he wasn't giving her that look—no, there it was. That odd, expressionless judge-y thing. *Fine.* She wasn't going to let him get to her. "Hi, Nadia. Hi, Tucker. Are you excited about the game?"

"I guess," Nadia said.

"Not a football fan?" Harley asked. "My favorite part is

the cheering. I like to cheer. Loudly. It's one of the few times you can yell at the top of your lungs and no one can stop you."

Nadia's shy smile grew. "Really?"

"Um, *really*. I can show you if you like?" Harley paused, giving Coach Grumpy-pants McBride the briefest of looks. "They're welcome to sit with us. Unless they're sitting someplace else?"

Where did his children sit during games? He was on the field—they wouldn't sit there, would they? Where else? Crossvine Creek was safe, sure, but that didn't mean she'd recommend letting Nadia and Tucker run around unattended for the entirety of the game.

"Normally, they sit with Mrs. Reed but she's under the weather—"

"She's sick." Nadia frowned, staring into the nearly packed stands with wide-eyed apprehension.

"Well that settles it." Harley took her hand. "You and Tucker should sit with me and Autumn and yell for the Wild Cats. As loud as you can."

"Can I, Daddy?" Nadia asked.

"Can I sit with my friends, instead?" Tucker asked, pointing at a group of boys sitting together in the bleachers. "I won't go anywhere. If I need something, I'm sure I'll be able to find Miss Harley—yelling."

"Oh, yeah, they're hard to miss," Noah added. "Noah Contreras." He held out his hand. "I don't think we've met."

"Probably not." Coach McBride shook hands with Noah. "Not unless you have a son on the team?" Josh McBride had the nerve to look remotely pleased to meet Noah. Come to think of it, he wasn't giving Autumn the whole judge-y look either.

"Nope." Noah held both hands up. "No kids. Not yet."

"Dad?" Tucker asked, nodding to his friends—who were all yelling his name and waving him over.

"Fine. Have fun." But Josh McBride's gaze stayed fixed on his son until the boy was safely seated in the bleachers. Then those bright blue eyes slammed into her. "Are you sure, Miss Welsh? I wouldn't want to impose."

"I'm absolutely certain, Mr. McBride." She was proud of how well she imitated his rather cool tone of voice. "Nadia and I will be just fine. We'll even have fun. Won't we, Nadia?"

Nadia was all smiles as she looked up at her father. "Please, Daddy."

Harley didn't blame the giant man for almost melting right then and there. Nadia was the most adorable little girl in the world. And her smile? Well, it could outshine the sun. He stooped to kiss her on the top of the head. "All right. You be good for Miss Welsh."

Nadia's little fingers tightened around Harley's. "I will."

"We're good?" Harley asked, waiting for his nod, before heading toward the bleachers. She looked down at Nadia. "I bet we can yell so loud, your daddy will be able to find you

SASHA SUMMERS

in the crowd."

"Think so?" Nadia asked.

"I know so." Harley grinned, holding tightly to Nadia's hand as they made their way into the stands to the stadium seats their father had 'saved' until they arrived. "Hey, Dad." She leaned forward, kissing her father's cheek. "I brought a friend. Nadia, this is my father. He's an artist, too."

But Nadia was content to stand behind Harley, peeking around her legs to murmur, "Hi."

"Glad you're sitting with us," her father said. "I hope Harley warned you, though. She gets awful loud when the game starts."

Nadia nodded.

"I told her, Dad. What's the fun in football if you don't yell?" Harley sat, scooching closer to her father so Nadia could squeeze in between her and Autumn. "Good?"

Nadia nodded again.

Harley tucked the fleece blanket over them. "Glad I brought this with me. Nice and toasty? It's chilly tonight." She tapped Nadia on the nose. "We don't want your nose turning blue."

Nadia giggled.

"This is my favorite time of the year," Harley added. "It's never *really* cold in Texas."

"Right." Noah held up the blanket. "This is just for show."

Autumn giggled. "It's cozy."

46

"It *is* cozy," Harley said. "And the big Fall Festival and all the fun stuff starts soon."

"What fun stuff?" Nadia asked, her big blue eyes peering up at her.

"Oh gosh, Nadia, I don't even know where to start," Harley said, tapping a finger to her chin. "Well, this weekend Mr. Krieger starts selling pumpkins out at his farm. We always go super early—so we can get the best pumpkin. Or two. Or three."

"Or five." Her father leaned forward, giving Nadia a wink. "Or more."

Nadia leaned against Harley, but she smiled. "That's a lot of pumpkins."

"Harley and Autumn paint some, carve some, bake some…you name it," her father added.

"Paint them?" Nadia asked.

"Definitely." Harley leaned down to add, "You'll get to paint your very first pumpkin in class next week."

Nadia's smile grew. "Will we get to use the Mr. Potato Head pieces?"

"These are for Mr. Krieger's Farm, but I'll make sure you get a set. Or two." Harley made a mental note to put some aside just for Nadia. "Then there are hay rides and scarecrow making and the Fall Festival." Harley ticked off each item on her fingers. "And the corn maze and pie-eating competition."

Nadia looked impressed.

"I know." Harley had to smile at the little girl's expression. "It's a whole lot of fall goodness."

Once the game started, Harley did her best to make things as fun as possible for Nadia. When she'd been little, it had been Autumn who'd coaxed Harley out of her shell. Harley had never quite acquired Autumn's carefree zest for life, though. While Autumn had a sock drawer full of wildly patterned and seasonal knee socks, Harley didn't even own a pair. Autumn was always spackled with paint, her hair in a messy bun, with a winning grin and radiating enthusiasm—people just loved her. Harley, on the other hand, felt out of sorts if she wasn't put-together and professional.

New York had driven that home. Or rather, Oliver had. To be a serious artist, you had to be serious. *Not that he'd wanted me to be an artist.* He'd been indulging her, wooing her, until she "snapped out of it" and realized what he had to offer was far more stable than counting on succeeding in an industry flooded "with real talent" and "the competitive spirit she clearly lacked."

He'd been right—about the competitive part. The dig about real talent had hurt.

Coming home, opening Welsh Studios with her sister, had filled the hole in her heart. Here, things made sense. Here, she had value, just as she was. That was why she loved working with her sister so much—Autumn never let Harley shy away from things or doubt herself. Her sister was always there for her, her own personal cheerleader. Her father, too. Neither one of them had pushed or asked questions she wasn't ready to answer when she'd come back from New York, heartbroken and shell-shocked.

She sensed that in Nadia. The same sort of fragility that needed love and protecting until she was strong enough to stand on her own two feet. It had taken Harley a good six months to feel grounded and steady again. But Nadia was young. For all the comments about kids bouncing back and being resilient, it would take time, support, and, when possible, good old-fashioned fun.

Like now.

Her father's clapping pulled her back to the present— alerting her to a Wild Cat player tearing down the field, running, full speed, for the goal post and a touchdown. Harley grabbed Nadia's hand, waited for the little girl to smile, and said, "Ready?"

Nadia giggled, her shoulders scrunched up as she nodded.

"Go!" Harley yelled. "Go, go, go!"

"Woohoo!" Autumn added.

Nadia looked at her. "Now?"

"Whenever you want. Here. Stand up so you can let it all out." Harley helped Nadia stand on the bench beside her. "Take a deep breath in and let it all out—so the whole team can hear you."

Nadia sucked in a deep breath. "Run, run, ruuun," she yelled, stretching the last word out so long and loud that her lungs had to be out of air as her voice faded away. When she was done, she looked Harley's way for approval.

"That was *awesome.*" Harley gave her a high five. "Everyone heard you."

"And look, Nadia." Harley's father leaned forward, pointing. "Your daddy did, too."

Nadia turned, waving wildly at the man with the wide eyes and huge grin. He was so caught up in his little girl's joy that, for a moment, the clipboard in his hand and the players waiting for his instruction seemed forgotten.

She might not be a fan of Coach Josh McBride, but she loved the way he adored his daughter. The fact that he was a massive, hulking, grumpy sort of man made his butterflies-in-the stomach-inducing grin that much more powerful. He wore such a startlingly genuine expression that Harley found herself returning the gesture, smiling from ear to ear. And she didn't like it. Or the butterflies. Or the odd tightness of her throat. Or the sudden warmth in her belly. Or the pressure against her chest...

But when Coach Blue-Eyes McBride's gaze shifted to her, all the tugs and flutters and flushing panicked her. She glanced around, searching for a focal point—and zeroing in on Nadia's shoelaces. They were tied, but that didn't stop her from straightening them. Anything to avoid Josh McBride, those blue eyes, that grin, and the extremely concerning reaction she was having to the man she did not— absolutely positively—have the slightest interest in. Beyond helping his precious daughter, of course.

THE GAME WAS a lock. His boys had played hard and they'd delivered. And, yes, the victory was all the sweeter because the town of Crossvine Creek was here to see it. Was he proud? Definitely. Of these boys. The progress they'd made since they'd started July two-a-day practices had blown him away. There was nothing more rewarding than seeing a team that's worked so hard get the win they deserved. If his boys kept playing like this, they might not have to wait until next year before they made it to state playoffs.

But the thing that stuck out in his mind most about this evening, blindsiding him? Seeing his little girl fearlessly cheering on the team—with Harley Welsh at her side. She hadn't been that openly joyful since before Lolly's passing and the move.

If he'd needed further proof that Nadia and Harley Welsh had a connection, that was it. Right there. All the yelling and clapping and smiling... Through most of the game, too. It was almost like the first bout of cheering had opened the floodgates of his little girl's enthusiasm.

"Well, well, Coach McBride," Bev Washington said as she came up to him, wearing Crossvine Creek purple and gold from head to toe. "That was some game."

He nodded, assuming 'some game' was a compliment.

"This is him, ladies," Bev said, standing aside so the similarly purple-and-gold-clad group of older women could give him an anything but subtle head-to-toe assessment. "Coach, this is some of the girls in my book club. Viola North, Jentina Ramos, and Cynthia Contreras. I've told them all about you—being my neighbor and a good father and new in town."

The longer the four women stared, the more uncomfortable he felt. Granted, they looked just like the sort of full-of-life and opinionated women Lolly would have chosen for friends… But that didn't make it better. As much as he'd adored his mother, she loved nothing more than being right in the middle of everyone else's business.

"Nice to make your acquaintances," he said, offering a smile he hoped didn't reveal the unease pricking at the base of his neck.

"And so polite," Mrs. Ramos said. "Bev said you were quite the gentleman."

"I hear you're single?" the older woman, wearing not only large purple-framed glasses but a gold feather boa around her neck, asked.

"Viola," Bev growled, blinking rapidly. "Behave."

"What?" Viola shrugged. "It's a yes or no question. I don't see a ring on those big hands of yours so I'm guessing it's a yes. Or are you one of those newfangled men who don't believe in wearing a wedding ring?"

He cleared his throat. "Widower." The ring had come off two years after Bethany's death and he still felt its absence.

The collective apologies and sympathetic sounds were

sincere.

"Oh. Well now," Viola said. "We all know how that feels. It's like getting the wind knocked out of you and not knowing which way is up."

Which was pretty much exactly how he'd felt.

"It gets easier—not better, but easier," Cynthia said, studying him a little more intently than the others. "They say that those who've truly loved once are more likely to find it again."

Considering he barely had ten minutes to himself each day, the likelihood of him finding time for a relationship was slim. That was, assuming he wanted a relationship. He didn't. But, from the continual staring of the women, he began to piece two and two together...and the level of his discomfort reached epic proportions.

What was it Lolly used to say? "I'm too old to break in a new man for myself but if I see two souls meant to be with one another, I'll do what I can to bring the two of them together."

"I'm happy," he said, the words thick and forced.

All four of the women nodded—but obviously none of them believed him.

"See that handsome young fellow out there, helping pick up all the equipment? That's Coach's son, Tucker. And that precious little thing?" Bev Washington said, pointing toward Harley and Nadia—Nadia who was sound asleep and curled up on Harley's lap. "That, right there, is his little one,

Nadia."

"She had such fun tonight," Cynthia said. "Harley is my... My... Well, Harley's father and I are a couple. Nadia was just a breath of fresh air—all energy and enthusiasm. Just adorable."

He couldn't help but smile then.

"She seems quite taken with Harley." Viola North's steely eyes fixed upon his daughter's sleeping form. "Can't say that I blame her. Good for Harley, too. Ever since she came back from New York, I've been hoping something or someone would fill the hole in that woman's heart."

He wasn't one to engage in gossip, but the older woman's words drew his attention. Was Miss Welsh nursing a broken heart? There was no way of knowing what a person was going through on the inside. Some people shut themselves off, others put on a smile and sought to protect and nurture other fragile souls needing comfort...like his daughter.

"Now, Viola," Cynthia said. "She's content. More than content, just the way things are."

"Content?" Viola snorted. "That's not happy now, is it?"

No, it wasn't. But it wasn't unhappy either. He went from studying his little girl to the woman holding Nadia. Harley was gently rocking where she sat, holding Nadia close, smiling and talking with her sister—all huddled together with a brightly colored thick fleece blanket over their legs.

A northerly gust rattled the chain-link fence and gave him the excuse he needed to wrap up this semi-interrogation of a conversation.

"It was nice to meet you all." He shifted from foot to foot. "I'd better get them home."

"Yes, sir. Don't want them catching a chill," Jentina Ramos agreed. "You take care, Coach. And keep up the good work."

"We'll see you soon, I'm sure." Viola North was all smiles.

The smiles added to his overall sense of dread and urged him to hurry home to find some much-needed peace and quiet. With a final wave, he went back to packing up his duffel bag and cleaning up trash until his team had all headed home. As he waved his final player off, he turned to find Tucker staring at the bleachers, tossing a football. *What is he staring at?* Of course. Harley Welsh. She was carefully walking down the steps of the bleachers, Nadia sound asleep in her arms. From the look on his son's face, Tucker's crush was growing.

He sighed, slung his duffel bag on his shoulder, and walked their way.

"She fell asleep," Harley whispered. "I don't know how, since we sort of made our own cheering section—"

"I noticed." He reached forward to take his sleeping daughter.

There was the slightest tilt of Harley's head—almost defiant—as she stepped down from the bleachers.

"What I mean is, I appreciate you including her to-night." He paused, his gaze bouncing from Harley Welsh to Tucker, who'd walked over to meet them. "I haven't seen Nadia that full of energy in a long time."

"Or that loud," Tucker added, yawning.

Harley's posture eased. "It was my pleasure. She's a good little cheerleader." She winked at Tucker then cleared her throat and asked, "I was wondering if you were planning to take Nadia and Tucker to Krieger's farm on Sunday?"

"Whose farm?" He shifted Nadia in his arms, holding the stadium gate open for her and Tucker.

"Oh, right. Yeah, Dad," Tucker piped up, yawning again. "Some of my friends are going. Sounds awesome."

"It is awesome." Harley nodded, grinning at Tucker. "You should go. All of you."

"To this farm?" It didn't sound all that awesome. Then again, this was his life now. He needed to engage. Small towns meant traditions and football…and farms. "Okay."

"Well, if you don't want to go or you're busy, I can take the kids." She tucked her hands into the pockets of her black-and-white coat.

"I appreciate the offer." He stopped underneath one of the light poles, glancing around the mostly empty parking lot. Small town or not, he'd feel better knowing she wasn't left alone after dark. "Where are you parked?"

"I'm over there." She pointed behind herself, waving at

the classic Ford Bronco with its lights on. "They're waiting. Autumn and Noah and Noah's mom, Cynthia, and my dad."

Right. He'd met Cynthia. Viola North's comment about Miss Welsh replayed in his mind, pulling his gaze back toward Harley. Someone had hurt her? Whether or not she was suffering from a hole in her heart, one thing was certain. She was...beautiful. And the tip of her nose was red and...cute. *I need a hobby.*

"Anyway, my whole family is planning to go in the morning. I can come pick them up and take them, if you'd like," she asked, shivering. "What time would be best for you?"

"I'll take them." He hadn't intended to snap. But his son's frown and the return of Miss Welsh's defiant chin-thrust said it all. He was really going to have to work on this accepting help thing. "But...can we meet you there? If that's not intruding on your family tradition?"

Her gaze met and held his. "It's not." She had more to say, he could tell, but Tucker's loud yawn stopped her. "How about around nine? I look forward to it." With a wave at Tucker and a smile his way, she turned to go.

Once they reached the Jeep, he opened the back door for Tucker then went around to the other side, taking care to gently ease Nadia into her booster seat.

"Daddy?" Nadia asked, her heavy-lidded gaze barely parting. "Did you hear me?"

"I heard you." He buckled her in, leaning in to press a kiss to her forehead.

"The whole town heard you, Squirt," Tucker said, laughing. "Are you going to be a cheerleader?"

"I don't know." Nadia smiled. "Miss Harley?"

Until then, he hadn't realized Harley Welsh was standing behind him.

"Hi, Nadia." She waved, slightly out of breath and red-cheeked.

"I like cheering." Nadia's head rested against the back of her booster seat, her eyelids drooping heavy.

"Me too." Harley stepped closer—so close he caught a whiff of perfume—something light and invigorating, yet feminine.

Which perfectly described Harley Welsh. *Maybe I just need sleep.* He ran a hand over his face, doing his best not to focus on the woman standing close beside him.

"I wouldn't be surprised if you were cheering in your dreams," Harley added. "Maybe, next week, we can do it again."

Even though his daughter's eyes drifted shut, the smile on her face was answer enough. "Night, Miss Harley."

"Night, sweet girl." Harley sighed, stepping back so he could shut the Jeep door. "Sorry. I'm sure you're eager to get them home."

Josh didn't say anything. Considering how tight his throat felt, he'd probably sound like he was angry. While he wasn't exactly happy about the effect this woman had on him, he wasn't angry. But if he didn't get a grip, he risked alienating the only person in Crossvine Creek that his daughter trusted.

"Here." Harley handed him a folded piece of paper. "It's a flier—with directions. For the farm. Autumn thought you might need it."

He eyed Harley's car, still parked some distance across the parking lot. "You ran?" he asked, looking pointedly at her heels. They weren't as high as the ones she'd worn at the art gala, but they'd be a challenge to run in. For that matter, they weren't exactly the sort of shoes to wear to a small-town football game either.

She looked down at her feet, then back at him. "I ran." She stomped one foot, then the other, wrapping her arms around her waist. "It's just... Well, now you won't forget or get lost." Beneath the fluorescent shine of the parking lot lights, her eyes were almost black.

Meaning she thought he'd back out? He wasn't exactly sold on the idea but he wouldn't back out. Still, he sighed. "Thanks."

"You're welcome. I promise, Nadia will have fun." She shrugged. "Who knows, you might have fun too."

He glanced down at the paper. "At Krieger Farms?" The question was weighted with skepticism.

She heard it and smiled. "Yes. It's not really fall until you pick out a few pumpkins now, is it?"

"I guess not." If he was being honest with himself, he'd admit he didn't know the first thing about any of this. Lolly had been the one who'd made holidays special. *Now it's up to me.* He folded up the flier and tucking it into his pocket. "I appreciate this." The instant his gaze collided with hers, he regretted it. "And tonight." He had a hard time not staring at her—and that smile.

Harley Welsh stepped closer. "Don't tell anyone, but Nadia is sort of my favorite, Coach McBride. I want her to be happy too—"

"I know." He cleared his throat. "I'm just overprotective. It's the way I'm wired."

"A father should be." Harley hugged herself more tightly. "Just remember, I'm on the same team. Team Nadia." Her smile grew. "Go team."

There was no way he could stop himself from smiling then—or chuckling.

For a split second, the air between them pulsed—a weighted, tangible thrum that charged the slight space between them. Not in a bad way. The exact opposite, in fact. The longer they stood there, smiling and staring, the stronger the sensation became. As much as he wanted to believe this had nothing to do with them and everything to do with their mutual devotion to Nadia, he knew better. This was different. Warm and fluid, rising up to flood him with...yearning. It had been so long since he'd felt anything like this... It was *unnerving.* He sucked in a deep breath and stepped back. "Thanks."

She blinked. "Yes...sure... You're welcome." Another blink. "See you...Sunday." And without another word, she ran across the parking lot to the car waiting for her.

He stared after her, processing. Reeling was more like it. He sucked in a few deep breaths of the crisp fall air to clear his head. Too bad it was scented with traces of Harley Welsh's perfume.

Chapter Four

HARLEY SIPPED HER hot chocolate, inspecting each and every pumpkin as she walked along the rows. On top of the ninety-plus pumpkins she and Autumn ordered from Mr. Krieger for their studio classes, her family always picked at least four for their home—one for each member of the family. As far back as she could remember, carving pumpkins had been just another way to kick off the long holiday season. From Halloween to Thanksgiving to Christmas, Crossvine Creek seized every opportunity to make each and every holiday a celebration.

"What about this one?" Autumn asked, pulling one hand from the pocket of her denim coveralls to point at a rather lopsided pumpkin with a flat face.

Cobie set about sniffing the pumpkin all over— determining whether or not the pumpkin was a good fit. Autumn swore her black Lab understood everything she said. There were times, like now, Harley agreed with her.

Baxter, Noah's little dog, followed suit. He circled the pumpkin, cocked his head to the side, then stared up at Autumn and Noah.

"Looks like you've got their approval." Noah chuckled.

"You did notice it's off center?" Harley smiled, knowing full well the pumpkin was Autumn's pick. She loved choosing the irregular ones—she said they inspired more creativity than 'any ol' perfect pumpkin.' Considering how many times they'd won the Crossvine Creek Holiday Yard Competition, there was no arguing with her logic.

"Yes. So what? I love it." Autumn stooped, cradling the large pumpkin against her chest.

"Nice socks," Noah said, catching a glimpse of Autumn's green socks covered in leering carved pumpkins. Autumn had a pair of seasonal knee socks for every season.

"Thank you." Autumn smiled up at Noah. "Someone special gave them to me."

"He sure did." Noah winked. "Need help with that pumpkin? It's bigger than you are."

Harley shook her head. "Aren't they adorable?" she asked the dogs, watching the interaction between their humans.

"A little too much sugar, if you ask me." Mr. Krieger was as grumpy as ever as he pushed his wheelbarrow between the rows. "You taking that one, Miss Welsh?"

"I am." Autumn nodded. "Thank you."

"Go on and put it in here and I'll take it up there for ya," Mr. Krieger barked. "Too many folks dropping them, wanting another, but expecting to not pay for the one they dropped. Figured this would put a stop to that nonsense."

Harley exchanged a smile with her sister. "Good plan,

Mr. Krieger."

He eyed the dogs as Autumn deposited the pumpkin, then pushed the wheelbarrow back down the row.

"You know, I have never seen that man smile." Noah shook his head.

"I have." Harley walked on, continuing to look for her pumpkin. "Believe it or not, he gives us special treatment. He always gives us one pumpkin for free."

Noah snorted. "Because you buy half of his crop, maybe?"

"Nadia is here." Autumn waved, her voice lowering. "With your dreamy coach."

Harley shot her sister a look. "You mean, her *father*?" After she'd run back across the parking lot last night, her heart hammering in her chest, she'd expected the ride home to be a stream of teasing and questions. To her surprise, no one had said a thing. It was bad enough that she was grappling with something she had never—*ever*—experienced before... But the loaded silence of their car ride? Well, that made it ten times worse.

She'd spent the rest of the night assuring herself that nothing had transpired between them. No weird awareness or invisible tether connecting them or electric jolt in the air. *None* of that happened. It hadn't happened then and it *wouldn't* happen today.

Today was about Nadia and Tucker and introducing them to one of Crossvine Creek's fall traditions and, hopefully, giving Nadia another day of fun.

There was a sharp tug on her heart when Harley saw the way Nadia was clinging to her father. Instead of looking around her, she was staring at the ground, doing her best to walk behind her father—almost hiding.

"Poor little thing." Autumn's words echoed exactly what Harley was thinking.

"I get the feeling there is so much more to the story." Harley glanced at her sister. "I just wish there was something I could do. For all of them." They'd been hurt. Her subtle questions about Lolly had told her that much. But she didn't dare push. Besides, she had a feeling that asking Josh McBride too many questions would only make him go out of his way to avoid her. For now, anyway.

Maybe, in time, that would change. But for now, Nadia needed her.

"I think inviting them here is a good start." Noah smiled at her. "You and your sister have a way of bringing joy into things. It won't be long before you win Nadia over. Likely, the whole McBride family."

Harley didn't miss the not-so-subtle jab of her sister's elbow into Noah's side. And she knew what it meant, too. "Autumn...please, please promise me you're not going to try to fix me up with Josh McBride. Please."

"I never said I was doing that." Autumn shrugged, glancing at Noah. "Did I? Say any of that?"

Harley sighed, knowing any protest would fall on deaf

ears. Once her sister had made up her mind, there was no changing it. Ever since Autumn and Noah had brought their father and his mother together, Autumn had taken on a new hobby—matchmaking. Harley had pointed out that there was a team of retired and elderly women already filling that role, but Autumn clearly wasn't taking the hint.

With another sigh, she headed down the row toward the McBride family.

"Hey, Miss Welsh." Tucker noticed her first, his cheeks red and his smile awkward. "Find a pumpkin?"

"Good morning." She beamed at them all, forcing herself not to linger on Josh McBride—his strong jaw or just how blue his eyes were in the bright morning sun. "I was waiting to pick one. I thought you all might be willing to lend a hand—or an eye?"

Tucker nodded.

She turned her attention to Nadia then, who'd emerged from behind her father and was staring up at her. "How about we find you the perfect pumpkin? And one for me, too?"

Nadia smiled. "Or two?" she asked, reaching out to her—her other hand still fiercely holding on to her father.

"Or two." She risked a quick glance at Josh McBride. He was, without a doubt, the tallest man she'd ever met. And broad. He was a coach—so it made sense that he took care of himself. Add the strong jaw, handsome face, and blue eyes and Coach McBride was, in fact, pretty dreamy.

Great. Dreamy? Thanks a lot, Autumn.

His brows rose, the corner of his mouth barely curling. "Two, huh?"

"We always get one for each member of the family," Harley said, taking Nadia's other hand. "And then we decorate them however we want."

"We need three?" Tucker asked.

"Maybe not *need*. That's up to you. You'll have to start your own tradition." Harley squeezed Nadia's hand. "That's the fun part. You see, Crossvine Creek does a monthly yard competition. Whoever's yard is the nicest or most decorated, gets a sign to display. Autumn, my sister, takes this very seriously." She winked at Nadia.

"Have you won?" Coach McBride asked.

"Every year for the last four years." Harley sighed. "Like I said, she takes it *seriously*."

The corner of his mouth ticked up a little higher but he didn't respond. If anything, he seemed to be lost in thought—until those blue, blue eyes swiveled her way and held.

No, no, no… This is not happening.

But it was. Again. And his gaze was more magnetic and far warmer this time. And she was growing warmer with each breath. His unflinching hold triggered a very real, very visceral response. Pressure and heat and attraction. Overwhelming attraction. Raw and fluid and…and… *It is so happening.*

"Where do we start?" Tucker asked. "I mean, there are lots pumpkins to choose from."

Breathe. Harley drew in a deep breath. *Stop staring.* She blinked. *Say something.* "Well, hot chocolate is always a good place to start." If she sounded a little breathless and weird, there was nothing she could do about it.

"Hot chocolate?" Nadia asked. "I love hot chocolate."

"Let's get you some." The sooner she found a way to defuse these beyond-bizarre feelings, the better. "That's another reason to come today. Arnie and Georgia Lane always bring out hot chocolate and donuts from the bakery in town." She did not look at Coach McBride. She couldn't. But she had a sneaking suspicion he was looking at her.

"Donuts?" Tucker asked.

"Tucker loves donuts," Nadia said. "Daddy says he might turn into one."

Harley chuckled, leading them toward the table the Lanes had set up beside the barn. There was a short line, but it was moving quickly.

"Good morning, Nadia and Tucker and Coach. Mind if we jump in?" Autumn asked, Cobie's leash in hand. "Hot chocolate makes everything better."

"You remember Cobie?" Harley asked, smiling down at Nadia.

Nadia was already speaking softly to the large dog. Cobie was all tail-wagging and happy sniffs.

"Morning," Noah said, shaking Coach McBride's hand.

"Who is this?" Nadia asked, studying Baxter but not making a move to touch the little dog. Unlike Cobie, Baxter took a while to warm up to people.

"This is Baxter," Autumn said. "Bax, this is Nadia and Tucker."

Baxter stood, sniffed the hands each child offered, then allowed Nadia to give him a scratch behind the ear.

"Wow, he likes you," Harley said. "Guess Baxter can tell how sweet you are."

Nadia's smile was broad and carefree. "I like you too, Baxter."

She heard Josh McBride's sigh and had a hard time fighting back a smile. The poor man had made it clear he had reservations about getting a dog and yet here he was, surrounded by well-behaved, impossible-to-resist canines that would only fuel Nadia and Tucker's desire for a dog of their own.

"I'm warning you now," Noah said to Josh McBride. "Once these two get started, there's no stopping them in the quest for the perfect pumpkin. You think this will be easy. But no. Apparently, it's not just a grab-and-go scenario."

Harley turned away at the first sign of Josh McBride's smile. She had to. Thankfully, Noah drew Josh into conversation. Football, no surprise. This season had the whole town buzzing. After all, Harley couldn't remember the last time their team had had this many wins. Now the two of them were talking about the players, the team, and their chances of progressing—giving Harley a chance to process some of the weirdness she was feeling.

"You should hunt pumpkins with us." Harley gave her sister an imploring gaze, but not because she wasn't perfectly capable of conversing with Josh McBride on her own. She was, one hundred percent. But it would be easier to have someone else converse with him—since he didn't seem all that inclined to say more than a few words to her. *And* there was the electric-shock-connection thing, on her part anyway. His whole expressionless thing made it hard to tell what he was thinking or feeling. Besides, she needed to focus on Nadia and Tucker. That was what this was all about. "Since you've already found yours."

Autumn's eyes narrowed slightly, but she was all smiles. "No worries. We're not going *anywhere*." The gleam in her older sister's eyes was not the least bit reassuring.

Overall, the morning went smoothly.

After the hot chocolate and donuts were consumed, Tucker, Nadia, and Harley headed straight into the pumpkin patch. She let them take the lead, pausing to listen as they discussed the pros and cons of a handful of pumpkins. Tucker wanted the biggest one he could find. Considering Mr. Krieger grew some monster-size pumpkins, she worried how his father would react. Nadia was another matter. As usual, she was quiet and contemplative. She'd pause, kneel, gently turning the gourd before standing and moving on.

"What are you looking for, Squirt?" Tucker asked. "You

are sure looking hard."

Nadia shrugged. "I dunno."

"I bet you'll know when you see it," Harley said.

"How long have they been doing this?" Josh asked, coming alongside her.

"Oh, gosh, always. Forever. I've only missed one—when I was living in the city. It was terrible." She laughed. "You never know how much you value little things, traditions and such, until they're gone, you know?" Of course, that seemed to be the wrong thing to say since Josh McBride's jaw was clenched so tight the muscle looked ready to pop.

"I do." The words were ground out. But he wasn't angry. Beyond the clenched jaw and gruff words, right beneath the surface of his brusque exterior, there was pain.

Without thinking, she placed her hand on his arm. Touch was a way to comfort people. It was something she would have done for anyone. But when the glacial indifference slipped, the hurt he hid so well was stripped bare for her to see. Whatever had happened in his past, it had left scars. Her hand tightened, holding on to his forearm—until the hurt faded and those blue eyes swept over her face. Searching. Curious. And absolutely mesmerizing.

HE'D SPENT THE last year offering comfort. He was a father. It was his job to comfort Tucker and Nadia. Especially

Nadia. It was up to him to ease their fears and assure them that everything would be all right—even when he had no way of knowing if that was true.

Nadia was fearful of crowds because she'd seen her grandmother collapse in front of her. It had been a normal trip to the grocery store, nothing special. But Lolly's stroke had left Nadia alone with strangers until he'd been able to get to her. Now, it didn't take much for all the noise and fear and panic to creep up on his little girl—especially when they went someplace new. There were times he woke up now and then to find Nadia at his bedside because she needed to make sure that her daddy was still there.

Harley Welsh didn't know any of that but she was offering comfort all the same. And he needed it—ached for it, deep in his bones. The sympathy in her big brown eyes rolled over him, easing him. He might be the parent but there were times when all he wanted was for someone to hold him close, to tell *him* things would be okay—even for a second.

The shift of the wind blew the silky strands of Harley's hair across his arm and hand. It was the softest touch, a whisper, but it was enough. His need for comfort gave way to a wave of awareness that was no less disconcerting than it had been before. With any luck, she wouldn't hear his heart hammering away.

He tore his gaze from hers but her gentle grip tightened—tempting him to stay right where he was. What was happening? He wasn't needy. He didn't let his emotions dictate his behavior. This didn't make sense.

"Daddy, look," Nadia said. "Look."

Harley's hand slip from his arm, sending a ripple over each and every nerve along his arm. Breathing a little easier now that her touch was gone.

"Oh, that *is* a good one." Harley crouched by Nadia.

Josh swallowed hard, flexed his hand, and moved to the other side of the pumpkin. Whatever might help stop *that* from happening again. "This one?" he asked, swallowing again. "What is it that you like about it?" Considering she'd been walking the rows for almost an hour, it seemed like a fair question.

"I don't know." Nadia smiled up at him. "I just like it."

"Well, that's good enough for me." He scooped up the pumpkin.

"Don't drop it, Daddy." Nadia clasped her little hands together. "It's perfect."

"I won't," he said, noting just how imperfect the pumpkin was. "Are we all done?" *Please, let this be done.*

"No." Tucker pointed across the rows. "I want one of those."

Josh looked in the direction his son was pointing. "The ones you could turn into a playhouse for your sister?"

"Those are Mr. Krieger's prize pumpkins." Harley laughed.

Her laugh was husky. Tempting. *Knock it off.*

"What prize?" Nadia asked.

"Oh, there's a contest at the Pumpkin Patch Fall Festival for the biggest pumpkin. And then the winner goes on to the state fair. Mr. Krieger's won a few times. Did you see all those blue ribbons framed in the barn? He won those," Harley said, smoothing a hand over Nadia's hair. "I'm not sure he sells those, Tucker. And, besides, your dad is right. I don't know how you'd get one of those into your Jeep, let alone home and carved."

Tucker shrugged. "Plus, all the seeds and gunk inside. There would be tons of it."

"There is that," Harley agreed. "You'd have a year's supply of roasted pumpkin seeds though."

"Roasted?" Nadia asked. "You don't plant them?"

"If you want a garden." Harley looked his way. "Are you going to plant a garden, Coach Mc—"

"Josh," he interrupted her, doing his best not to snap or frown or get lost in her eyes.

Harley blinked.

"My name." *Great job on not snapping.* He sighed.

Harley blinked again, her cheeks going red when her gaze slipped to his mouth.

That did it. All he could do was stare...his heart thumping, hard and fast, against his rib cage. What was he supposed to do now? Because he wanted to do something. He was either going to give in and buy whatever pumpkins his kids wanted so he could get out of there *or* he'd throw the pumpkin he was holding over his shoulder and pull Harley Welsh into his arms...

He swallowed a groan. Now he couldn't stop thinking about it. Harley. In his arms. And it wasn't for comfort... The reason didn't matter.

What was he doing? He wasn't interested in a relationship. He didn't have time for that sort of...complication. Life was complicated enough.

Harley was a good person, kind and patient and oh so beautiful... *Not helping.* After losing Lolly and the trauma of this move, Nadia needed someone. That someone was Harley.

If something went wrong between him and Harley, Nadia might lose Harley too. He wouldn't do that to his daughter. Harley Welsh was off-limits. Starting now. He turned away from her and stared, blindly, over the rows of pumpkins.

"There are more over here," Noah called, waving Tucker over. "Behind the barn. Pumpkins as far as the eye can see."

Great.

"Did you hear that?" Nadia asked. "Come on, Daddy."

"But you still want this one?" Josh asked, following his children.

"Yep," Nadia said, taking Harley's hand and half-running, half-skipping after Autumn and Tucker.

"How are you settling in to small-town living?" Noah asked, a dog leash in each hand.

"It's different." He shrugged. "Not bad. Just different."

"I was born here but I've been traveling the last few years. I'd forgotten about all the good there is here. The people—community. Always willing to lend a hand."

Josh chuckled. "Some more than others." He shook his head.

"Yeah, I spied the book club ladies talking to you at the game. Viola, Bev and Jentina. Even my mom, Cynthia." Noah shot him a sympathetic grin. "You've probably already figured it out, but I feel like I should warn you anyway. You're definitely high on the list of their priorities."

He frowned. "Meaning?"

"Well, you're single." Noah paused while Cobie nosed around in a bush. "For some reason, they feel compelled to get everyone married and settled."

He'd figured as much. Still, he'd hoped. "Great."

"I know. That's why I'm warning you." Noah grinned. "It's one of their hobbies, I guess. Reading, knitting things, cooking, and playing matchmaker."

"If I want to give them a hard pass, who should I talk to?" He smiled as Nadia spun, her hands over her head, talking to Harley.

"Well, you can try Bev Washington, your neighbor." Noah shook his head. "Pretty sure it won't do you any good, though."

When Josh had started looking for a place to live, Crossvine Creek had fit the small-town, look-out-for-your-neighbor, good schools, and low crime profile he'd wanted. He'd had several solid offers—he had a reputation for building highly competitive teams—but none of them could compare with Crossvine Creek's. But he'd taken the job thinking that looking out for your neighbors meant cutting one another's grass or asking after one another's welfare— maybe the occasional neighborhood get-together. Fending off a group of matchmaking retirees had never crossed his mind. That hadn't been included in the information packet the chamber of commerce had sent to him—with a warning label.

Tucker was waving at a couple of boys about his own age. His son had never met a stranger. He was easygoing, low-maintenance, and super smart. Seeing him laughing with kids his age warmed him through. But…now that Tucker's friends were here, their departure would get pushed back.

And that's okay. It's not like they had a million things to do. His kids were happy. That was about as good as it got.

Josh liked Noah well enough. It helped that he didn't have a son on the team, looking to befriend him in the hopes that his son would get more play time or their friendship would somehow influence things. He was always wary about that. It was just another part of the whole coaching thing but it tended to prevent him from getting too friendly with the parents.

At the sound of Nadia's laughter, Josh turned.

Harley, Autumn, and Nadia were sitting in tall grass, surrounded by blue and purple flowers. Harley was speaking animatedly, using her hands, her expressions fluid. She leaned forward, threading some of the flowers through Nadia's hair before sitting back to assess. After a quick once-over, she leaned forward and added more flowers.

"You're dating Miss Welsh?" Josh asked.

"Autumn? Yes." Noah's smile said it all. "I'm hoping we'll be more than just dating soon."

"Good luck." Josh meant it. He'd only had seven years with Bethany and he wouldn't trade a minute of it. Those were happy times—happy memories. Cancer was evil.

"You?" Noah asked. "It might just throw the matchmakers off if you had someone special."

"I've got my hands full as it is." He shook his head, his attention wandering back to Nadia. She stood, her hands full of the blue and purple flowers, and walked behind Harley. Just like with the pumpkin, his little girl took her time carefully threading the flowers into Harley's braid. She was smiling and talking with the Welsh sisters, but focused intently on what she was doing—without any sign of the tension or worry that so often seemed to weigh her down.

"I don't know if you're interested or not, but a few of the guys in town play poker every other Tuesday night," Noah said. "There's beer. And, even though I'm younger than most of the other players by twenty years, there's never a shortage of conversation and laughter."

"I appreciate the invite," Josh said. "It's hard, with the kids, but I guess I can ask Mrs. Reed if she's up for it."

"If not, I'm sure we can find someone else to watch the kids. That is, if you're interested?"

Josh nodded. "I'm interested." Guys' night? Poker? Why not?

Cobie chose that moment to jerk away from Noah, sprinting across the grass to Autumn, Harley, and Nadia. Nadia was giggling when Cobie covered her in kisses.

"Autumn said you were thinking about getting a dog?" Noah said.

"Thinking about it." But it was hard to remember why he was holding off when Nadia was so happy.

"They're a lot of work." Noah shrugged.

That was why. How was Josh supposed to juggle his job, his kids, and a dog? Nadia kept on giggling, tucking some flowers along Cobie's collar.

"I had no plans to get a dog," Noah said. "But then, I saw Baxter. And when I learned he'd been there so long, I knew he was going home with me. It just happens. He's a good dog. He's never even tried to bite my mother and she keeps stuffing him into sweaters." He shook his head.

Josh chuckled.

"Dad, Dad." Tucker came running across the field. "I found one."

"Are you sure?" Josh asked. "Is it small enough that I can carry it? Or do I need to rent a crane?"

"You're strong," Tucker said. "I think you can carry it."

"I appreciate the vote of confidence." He shook his head. "But—"

"I'm just teasing, Dad. It's not that big. But it does have all these cool bumps all over it. I'm going to make it into a zombie pumpkin." Tucker stared up at him, waiting for a reaction.

"Zombie pumpkin, eh?" He shrugged. "That's original."

"We have to go all out, Dad." Tucker kept on talking, pulling him away from Noah. "We should try to win this pumpkin contest."

"With zombie pumpkins?" he asked, loving Tucker's enthusiasm.

"Yeah. We can use the slimy guts and all of that. It'll be gross and cool." He paused. "We could ask both Miss Welshes if they'd help, too."

"You don't think we can carve a few pumpkins on our own?" Josh didn't know whether to be offended or amused. Come to think of it, when was the last time he'd actually carved a pumpkin? Lolly had special tools and stencils— things that made the whole process a little easier.

"No offense, Dad, but this is big. Like big-big. I say we call in some reinforcements."

"I don't know. From what I hear, the Welsh family has won this competition the last couple of years." He eyed the bumpy, discolored, lopsided pumpkin his son had led him to. "Okay, I can see where you got the zombie idea."

"I told ya." Tucker bent, lifting the pumpkin.

"Don't be disappointed if they're too busy, Tucker." He paused. "How about we trade?" Nadia's pumpkin was about half the size of Tucker's.

"Sure." After they traded pumpkins, Tucker made a beeline for his sister, the Welsh sisters, Noah, and the dogs. "We need help," Tucker said, plopping down in the grass beside Nadia. "Dad isn't so good at this sort of thing so I was hoping you could help me and Nadia with our pumpkins."

"I thought you were asking for help?" Josh had to laugh. "That was more like throwing me under the bus."

"Ooh, that does sound pretty dire." Autumn turned to Harley. "What do you think?"

"After that, how can we say no?" Harley was smiling, Nadia in her lap. Between the blue of her sweater and the blossoms in her hair, she was something to look at.

"Don't say no." Nadia looked up at Harley, tapping Harley's nose with a flower. "We will have fun, too."

"Yep. Zombie pumpkin fun," Tucker announced.

"Zombies?" Autumn grinned. "I'm so in. And I have just the right pair of socks for that."

"Only you would have zombie socks." Noah laughed.

Josh was aware that conversation was still taking place around him but he had no idea what was being said. The sun was out, the air was cool, his children were content, and, for just a minute, it didn't feel like he had the weight of the world on his shoulders. He liked seeing Tucker talk about his zombie idea. He loved how at ease Nadia was as she decorated Baxter's sweater with more flowers. For the first time, he felt good about his decision to move them here. This was good. A good day. He wanted more days just like this.

Harley's husky laugh filled the air, a hard-to-ignore reminder that he *might* want more than he was willing to admit.

Chapter Five

HARLEY HAD SPENT most of Sunday night, and several hours Monday night, sifting through her time with the McBrides at Krieger Farms. Nothing had made her happier than watching Nadia come to life—laughing and singing and making cornflower crowns, without a care in the world. Everything about their time together had eased some of her worry over the little girl and helped her understand a little more about what Nadia needed most: a playmate. The little girl was hungry for companionship but too uncertain to actively go after it. That's where Harley could help. Nadia needed someone who'd embrace her soft-spoken, contemplative, and creative ways and complement them. Harley had already started making a list of students she thought Nadia might mesh well with.

Tucker seemed to be finding his way. Harley recognized most of the boys he'd buddied up with—all goofy, energetic boys on the cusp of puberty who laughed over fart jokes and playing pranks.

Which left Josh McBride.

She blew out a deep breath.

What to do about Josh McBride?

She hadn't planned to touch him—he radiated a more hands-off vibe than the average person. But had that stopped her? No. The flash of pain in his brilliant blue eyes had made it *impossible* for her not to touch him. And that's when it had happened.

That *thing*.

That spark.

That magnetic force that kept her hand on his arm.

Once the initial shock had subsided, she'd expected him to pull away. The whole thing was...*weird*. Wasn't it? None of it *felt* normal. The current that arced between them the minute they touched? *Definitely not normal.*

But *he* hadn't shrugged her off or pulled away or given her a look or word of reproach, either.

It was impossible to know if she was the only one experiencing this emotions-in-a-blender—on high—until the world turned upside down thing. Josh McBride hadn't acted like the earth had moved under his feet. He hadn't acted differently at all. Which led her to believe that her touch did *not* leave him a hyperventilating jumble of feelings.

But since that *was* the effect he had on her, she needed to find a way to deal with it. She needed to spend less time thinking about how big and handsome this wounded man was and more time focused on helping his precious little girl. It would be hard not to notice that Josh was big and handsome—he was. So maybe, just to be safe, she shouldn't look at him unless she had to. Less looking meant less potential staring…

Bottom line, she wasn't going to let a few tingles get the better of her.

While she'd been tossing and turning and not sleeping, she'd come up with a plan. And, with Autumn's help, she'd located the very thing she needed to make that plan succeed. The notebook paper was soft from age and crinkled from all the times it had been stuffed into a jacket pocket or the bottom of a backpack—but it was still legible. Her mother had written some of it, her father, too. She and Autumn had added a few lines as well—their handwriting large and uneven, a reflection of most six- and seven-year-olds' penmanship. She had a to-do list to follow. Harley couldn't remember a time, when she'd been a child, when the list hadn't been placed, secured with magnets, to the family refrigerator every fall. It became a family tradition.

The year Harley had come home from New York, Autumn had used the list to lift her spirits. It had been her decision to come home, her decision to end her engagement to Oliver, but that hadn't meant her heart wasn't hurting. With Autumn and her father and the treasured list, Harley had been reminded of what mattered most in the world—the love and support of her family, here in her hometown.

It was just the thing for the McBride family. Especially Nadia. If Josh was agreeable, Harley would use it to help Nadia settle in. Pumpkin hunting, apple dumpling baking, crafts, festivals, hay rides filled the list, as well as so much more. Nadia and Tucker—and maybe Josh—would discover all the wonderful things to love about their new home. The list was clear, concise, and fun.

It does not include losing my heart to Josh McBride. She drew in a deep breath.

That was why she was here, parking her car in the parking lot of Crossvine Creek High School with four dozen donuts. She checked in at the front desk, pinned the visitor's badge on her burnt-orange sweater, and headed down the hall toward the gym.

The coach's office door was closed, so she knocked—ignoring the surge of anticipation and warmth in her stomach—and smiled at two students who walked by. She raised her hand to knock again—at the same time he opened the door.

"You knocked?" His blue gaze flitted from her hand, which was knocking on his chest.

Her cheeks were on fire. "Sorry…you opened the door."

"That's normally what I do when someone knocks." The corner of his mouth twitched.

"Right." She cleared her throat, not looking at his mouth or noting that the corner was starting to curl just the slightest bit. *No looking.* "This is for you."

He took the boxes of donuts. "All of them?"

She had to smile and glance his way then. "I suppose. I'd sort of thought you'd share them with the team, though."

Those blue eyes moved slowly over her face. Very slowly, pausing now and then.

"Do you have a minute?" It was suddenly very hard to breathe. "I wanted to talk to you about something. It won't take long."

He stepped aside so she could come in, his brow furrowing slightly, then closed the door behind her.

"Thank you." She inspected his office—versus inspecting him. "Did you have fun Sunday? I mean, I hope you all did."

He slid the box onto his desk and perched on the corner. "We did." Unlike her, he had no problem looking at her... It was just further proof that she was the only one suffering an extreme reaction to the other's presence. Which was good.

"Good." *Stop stalling.* "I have an idea. For Nadia. A sort of welcome to Crossvine Creek." She pulled the list from her pocket. "You see, growing up, my family had a checklist—a sort of countdown to the holidays—and the Annual Pumpkin Patch Fall Festival. It's a big deal."

He took the list and laid it on his desk, gently smoothing the paper.

"I thought it might be something your family would find useful." She waited while he continued to study her list. "You don't have to, of course. It's just, being new, it's easy to miss things that might be a good way to connect with the community."

He glanced her way. "This looks like a lot of connecting."

He does have a sense of humor. She giggled, nervous. *It's not that funny.* But she giggled some more.

And he smiled.

It was some smile. *People smile all the time.* Just because it was him smiling... She focused on a framed team photo until the surge warmth and sudden crush of awareness was tolerable. One smile was not going to derail her from doing what she was here to do. Not in the least. "So...what do you think?" She risked another look.

He was still smiling. The corners of his eyes crinkled when he smiled. And he had a dimple. No, correction, two dimples. It was, honestly, the best smile. Maybe ever.

"Can I get a copy of this?"

She blinked. "A copy?"

"For me and the kids to follow?" He stood, seeming to take up far more space now that he was towering over her.

"Oh, well...I suppose." She swallowed, bracing herself for his response as she said, "I'd thought maybe I could act as your tour guide or event coordinator?"

He looked confused. Then wary. "Miss Welsh—"

"Harley," she interrupted. "If I'm going to call you Josh, you are going to call me Harley."

"Fine." He cleared his throat, and glanced her way. "Harley."

And just like that, all the tingles and awareness and tightness doubled... Or quadrupled. *Whatever.* The simple act of saying her name shouldn't send her into a tailspin.

"So…"

"You have this kind of time?" He focused entirely on her list.

"I do. It's only a month. And my family still does all of these things every year. It's tra—"

"Tradition." He nodded. "I've been hearing that word a lot."

"Small towns take a lot of pride in them." On the far wall, she noticed several framed newspaper articles and a grouping of family photos. One of Nadia, one of Tucker, and one of the kids with an older woman. She had the same blue eyes and wide smile. "It's one of the things that makes the community so close-knit, I think. Celebrating things together." She paused. "My guess is that it's one of the things you were probably looking for when you moved from the big city to Crossvine Creek?"

"It was." His attention shifted back to her. "I'll think about it."

"Of course." Her disappointment was unexpectedly sharp. "You know I think Nadia hung the moon, and the stars too, so this isn't just a way to bring her joy. I get a fresh look at things, through her eyes. I don't know if that makes sense or not…"

"It does." He ran a hand along the back of his neck. "And thank you, for the donuts yesterday. Arnie told me you picked up the bill."

"I figure offsetting your donut fund might cover your dry

cleaning. To get the pumpkin latte smell out of your things."
She shrugged. "Personally, I think pumpkin latte smells
delicious."

"As a drink, maybe. As a cologne? Not so much." One
eyebrow rose.

"Well, I still feel terrible about it. It was an accident."

"I'm the one who should apologize." He shook his head,
those blue eyes meeting hers again. "I'd had a rough morning
already, and the coffee just added to it. It's Nadia. School.
She's having a hard time. Well, you know…it was just one
more thing. Still, I had no right to be so—"

"Rude?" she asked. "Grumpy? Surly? Oh, wait, hostile?"

His smile was slow—and absolutely devastating. "All
that?"

Breathe. Relax. She'd come in here knowing full well she
could handle him…this… Her reaction to all of him. She
could do this. *Doubtful.* "All that. And more. You left and I
spent the rest of the morning feeling guilty and upset and a
little bit angry."

"Angry?" He crossed his arms over his chest—drawing
her attention to his arms. Thickly muscled arms. Like tree
trunks. What were those giant trees? Redwoods? Yes. That
was it. Josh McBride was the human equivalent to a giant
redwood tree. "About?" His smile seemed a little brighter—
and far more devastating.

"Well…" Her hands fluttered in agitation. "Maybe your
bad mood rubbed off when I tripped."

"You're welcome for that." Was he teasing her? "Better to bump into me than fall on the floor."

He was right. Better to be held in those arms against that wall of a chest than be sprawled out on the floor. *Oh, enough.* It was time to leave. "Fine." Another weird hand flutter and she was reaching for the door. "Thank you for breaking my fall. And I accept your apology for being grumpy—"

"And rude. And, what else?" He *was* teasing her. And enjoying it. "Surly, I think."

"Don't forget hostile." Her hand gripped the doorknob. "I have to get to the studio. Nadia's class will be there shortly."

"I know. She loves Tuesdays and Thursdays best." He eyed the paper again. "If you're sure you have time, and having us tag along won't be a bother, I'd appreciate this. The kids will too. We can try the first item on your list, pumpkin carving, and see how it goes.

She was far more excited than she'd expected. "Pumpkin carving." She stepped toward him but slammed on the brakes before she made the cataclysmic mistake of actually hugging him. Still, she was close—too close.

Like before, he seemed to be doing an inventory of her face. "Really." The word was low and soft—not at all what she was used to from Josh McBride. *Josh.* Who took another step toward her. Then another.

Instead of making the prudent choice of stepping back, she didn't move.

"You've got something." He reached up, his fingers gently sliding through her hair. "Right here." But his hand stayed, hovering close by her cheek.

"I brought the grade reports." The door opened behind her, slamming into the wall. "Looks like we're all clear... Oh, sorry."

Harley stepped back, spinning to face the new arrival. "Hi, Bernie." Bernie Ulrich had been the assistant coach since Harley had attended high school here. "I was dropping off some donuts for the team." She pointed at the boxes.

The word 'donut' caught Bernie's full attention. "Well, now, isn't that kind of you. Cream-filled too." Bernie rubbed his hands together.

"This was...in your hair," Josh said. A long piece of maroon yarn dangled from between his fingers.

"Oh." Her laugh was breathless. "I guess I'll need to fix my knit hat." She took extra care not to touch him. *Why didn't I let him throw it away? It's not like I need the thread.* "Okay. I...I'll see you tomorrow night then. Pumpkin carving." With another bizarre hand flutter, she left—her heart beating so hard and fast she feared the sound would echo down the school hallway.

Josh regretted his decision the moment she walked out of his office—not the idea of it or the spirit of kindness in which the offer had been made, though. No, it was because he was putting himself in a situation he might not be able to control, a situation that might test his control over his feelings.

Still, it wasn't like he could pretend Harley didn't exist. There were reminders everywhere.

Bernie had gone on and on about Harley's thoughtfulness, mentioning her donut delivery to everyone and anyone he happened to see.

After work was no better. Nadia came home full of stories about art class. Before, it wouldn't have bothered him. Now? It didn't *bother* him. But every time Nadia said Miss Harley this or Miss Harley that, he could feel the slide of her silky hair across his fingertips or the widening of her gaze as she'd stared up at him in his office.

She'd seemed...surprised.

I know the feeling.

Wednesday morning meant a chaotic routine. Unlike Tuesday or Thursday, Nadia did everything in her power to get out of going to school. She didn't have a full-blown tantrum but her soft sniffles and eyes full of tears weren't any easier to deal with. He left her at the elementary school and walked across the field to the high school, hoping the day would get better.

It might have been his imagination, but Bernie seemed to pop into his office a few more times than usual. And each time, Bernie seemed disappointed. Josh didn't acknowledge it, but he knew what Bernie was after—no Harley, no donut delivery.

After practice he headed home, took a shower, and came downstairs to make dinner.

"Doorbell," Tucker called out. "Dad?"

Josh draped the kitchen towel over his shoulder, walked down the hall, and opened the front door. "Harley?"

"Ooh, what's for dinner?" She smiled up at him, like showing up on his front porch with a bulging canvas bag hanging from one shoulder and a box tucked under her other arm was the most normal thing in the world.

"Stew…" He took the box.

"Thank you." She stepped inside. "Perfect stew weather." She paused, giving him an odd look. "But, if there's not enough, I can eat when we're done. No worries."

"Done?" he asked.

She stopped. "Pumpkins? Tonight? No?"

"Pumpkins." *Pumpkin carving.* She'd said something on her way out of the office. Something about tomorrow night. *Which was tonight.* If he'd been paying less attention to *her* and more attention to what she'd said, he might have made note of when they were starting. "Right. I remember." He shook his head. "But I probably should look a little closer at that list."

She laughed. "Good idea."

"Miss Harley?" Nadia's voice carried down the hall, echoed by the beat of her footsteps. "What are *you* doing here?"

"I'm here to *surprise* you." Harley glanced his way. "Surprise. We're going to decorate your pumpkins."

"We are?" Nadia clapped her hands.

"After dinner," he added.

"Yes, after dinner." Harley nodded, tapping Nadia on the nose. "Brain food."

"Which there is plenty of," Josh whispered. "Please, join us."

"So you didn't remember?" She waited for him to shrug. "Only if you're sure."

"I'm sure." He wasn't sure—about any of this.

"Thank you," Harley whispered back. "It smells really good."

"What are you whispering?" Nadia asked, whispering.

"If they're whispering, they don't want us to hear them." Tucker gave him a long, thoughtful look. Then Harley, too. "You need help, Miss Harley?"

"I do." Harley's kid-caught-with-the-cookie-jar expression was one of his favorite Harley expressions so far. "I might have brought a *few* extra pumpkins with me."

"How many is a few?" Josh asked.

"You might want to help him," Harley admitted with a smile. "Thank you for offering, Tucker."

His son smiled in response, a rush of color flooding Tucker's cheeks. *I know the feeling.*

"We can serve dinner, Daddy," Nadia offered.

Tucker nodded. "Miss Harley needs a spot."

Harley glanced at the nicely set table. "I hate to be a bother—"

"You're not. There is plenty," Josh assured her.

While he and Tucker unloaded the additional five pumpkins Harley had brought with her, Harley and Nadia added another place setting and served up bowls of stew.

"I helped make the rolls," Nadia was saying as he pushed the front door closed behind him. "I like to help cook."

"I do too," Harley said, carrying a basket full of golden-topped dinner rolls to the table. "It's one of my favorite things to do. And the rolls look perfect."

"Thank you." Nadia smiled, climbing into her chair.

"We brought in all the pumpkins." Tucker shook his head, taking his seat at the table. "There's sure a lot of them."

"Cleaned Mr. Krieger's farm out, didn't you?" Josh teased, passing the basket of rolls around the table.

"Almost," Harley said. "I might have left one. Or two."

Dinner was full of good conversation and comfort food. He sat back while his kids chatted away with Harley. Harley shared stories about her family, especially her sister Autumn, and all the mischief they'd gotten into as children. It had been a long time since there'd been so much laughter at the dinner table.

"How do you like Crossvine Creek?" Harley asked, helping clear off the table.

"It's okay," Tucker replied.

Nadia frowned.

"You know what?" Harley asked, putting a bowl in the dishwasher. "Moving and being someplace new can be hard. I was certain I needed to go on to bigger and better things when I grew up. I was going to be a fancy artist, live in New York, wear a lot of black…" She broke off, laughing as she continued rinsing off plates. "That was an adjustment."

"Why?" Nadia asked. "You didn't make any friends?"

He and Harley exchanged looks.

"I made friends," Harley answered. "It wasn't easy. I was shy—like you. Sometimes I had to make myself talk to people and smile."

"How?" Nadia asked.

"Promise you won't laugh?" Harley leaned forward.

Nadia leaned in, too. "I promise."

Josh stopped loading the dishwasher, curious to hear what advice Harley was going to give his daughter.

"I practiced in the mirror." Harley wrinkled up her nose, waiting.

"You did?" Nadia asked.

"That way, when someone looked at me or smiled at me or started up a conversation, I could think about what I'd practiced." Harley shrugged. "It helped me."

Nadia was quiet, considering Harley's suggestions.

"Why did you come back?" Tucker asked.

At this point, Josh didn't bother pretending he wasn't listening. He turned, watching her while she thought over her answer. It was clear she was figuring out just what to say.

She smiled. "I realized I had everything I needed and wanted right here."

He may not know her all that well, but he knew that wasn't one of her genuine smiles. He remembered Viola North's words at the football game. But Harley's past was none of his business.

"I'm glad you're here," Nadia said. "We can do pumpkins."

"Yes, we can," Harley agreed. "I brought newspaper in my bag. We'll want to spread it out all over the back porch." She pointed at her bag. "And I brought some of the Mr. Potato Head pieces too. In case we don't want to make all the pumpkins into zombies."

It took almost two hours to get four of the seven pumpkins cleaned out and ready for the front porch. Two were carved zombies, one was brightly painted, and one had a cheerful Mr. Potato Head face in place. Harley had more patience than he thought was humanly possible. He was ready to throw in the towel after the second pumpkin but Harley kept at it.

"Now, try one." Harley slid the toasted seeds from the parchment-lined pan into a pumpkin bowl. "I promise they're yummy."

"You first, Daddy. They were slimy." Nadia looked up at him, flinching from the remembered slime of the pumpkin's insides.

Harley, Tucker, and Nadia all watched him as he popped several seeds into his mouth. "These are good. Better than what you can buy in the store." He ate a few more.

"Of course." Harley shook her head. "These are homemade. If you want, I can pack them up so you can have them for a snack later this week."

After a moment's hesitation, Tucker ate some. Then Nadia. Harley's smile was nothing short of victorious.

Josh had been so caught up in the evening, he'd lost track of time. "Nadia, it's time to get ready for bed."

"Okay, Daddy." Nadia smiled. "And tomorrow I get to see you again, Miss Harley."

"Yes, you do." Harley grinned and then ate a pumpkin seed. "And you'll get to paint your very own little pumpkin to bring home."

"Oh good. I was worried we wouldn't have enough pumpkins." Josh smiled, scooping Nadia into his arms. "You start getting ready too, Tucker."

Tucker sighed but did as he was told. "Night, Miss Harley."

"Night, Tucker. I like how your zombie idea turned out."

Tucker smiled, his cheeks going red, and ran up the stairs. His son had it bad.

"I'll clean up," Harley offered, taking in the mess.

"I've got this." He shook his head, smiling when Nadia rested her head against his chest. "Tonight was fun."

"So, a good *surprise?*" she asked, her brown eyes meeting his.

One look and he was done. After spending the entire evening avoiding any lingering gazes or accidental touches—the jolt that passed between them was as startling as ever. *A good surprise?* Everything about her was a surprise.

"Yes." Nadia yawned. "Are you coming to Daddy's game? We can cheer together again?"

"Hmm, I will let you know." Harley reached out, rubbing Nadia's back. "Have sweet dreams." Her eyes found his again. "Thank you for dinner. And the rolls. Next time, I'll have to cook."

He liked the sound of that a little too much.

"Okay," Nadia said.

"I'll go. You have your hands full. Literally. There's no need to wait on me. I'll pack up my stuff and let myself out." She started collecting her supplies before he could respond. "Night, Josh."

"Good night, Harley," he murmured, pausing long enough to see if she'd look his way.

She didn't.

Since Nadia was falling asleep in her bath, he cut it short. She couldn't keep her eyes open long enough for him to finish her favorite bedtime story either. He tucked her in, turned off the lights, cracked the door, and made sure the hall night-light was on.

"You good?" He stuck his head in Tucker's room.

Tucker was sitting up, a comic book open on his lap. "What do you think of Miss Harley?"

Josh had a feeling this was going somewhere so he sat on his son's bed. "She's nice."

Tucker shot him a disbelieving look. "Come on, Dad. Yeah, she's nice but...I think she's really pretty." He paused, crossing his arms over his chest.

He nodded.

"*Really* pretty."

He nodded again.

"And I think she likes us. Me and Nadia, I mean." Tucker closed his comic book. "You should try being nicer to her."

Josh swallowed down a laugh. "I'm not being nice to her?" His son couldn't understand the risks involved with being nicer to Harley.

"Sort of." Tucker shrugged. "But not enough. I like her."

"You're going to have to give me a little more to go on, Tucker. Nicer, how?"

"I don't know. Do you like her? You seem sort of...I don't know, weird...when she's around." Tucker looked up at him again.

Weird was a pretty accurate description. "So, I need to stop being weird?"

Tucker took a deep breath. "Yeah."

Josh cleared his throat. "I'll try."

His son smiled. "Good." He flopped back on his pillows.

"The zombie pumpkins were a pretty good idea, weren't they?"

Josh ruffled his son's hair. "They were."

"Because I'm a creative genius." Tucker yawned. "That's what Miss Harley said."

He stood and turned off the lights. "Time for this creative genius to go to bed."

"Night, Dad."

"Night." He pulled the door closed and headed back down the stairs to find Harley downstairs, cleaning. "Harley."

She froze, caught in the act. "You weren't supposed to come down yet."

He laughed. "I do live here."

"I know. And the place is almost back to being livable." Hands on hips, hair escaping from the twist on top of her head, she assessed the room. "At least, it's better than it was. Yes?" She turned, smoothing a hand over her hair, and waited for his answer.

"Much." The minute their gazes met, the room began to shrink.

Now that there were no kids or pumpkins or activities or distractions, resisting his instinctual stop-and-stare-at-Harley thing presented a problem. It would be one thing if he was alone in this but…he was pretty sure he wasn't.

If she didn't feel this tension between them, she wouldn't be acting as rattled as he was.

Every time the two of them were together, he found it harder to pretend the invisible thread binding them together wasn't being reeled in…inch by inch.

"It's late." Which was a fact—and also a hint for her to leave before there was a repeat of what had happened Tuesday morning. In his office. Right before they'd been interrupted. This time, Bernie Ulrich wasn't going to walk in. And from the exhausted state of both kids, they were probably already sound asleep. Which meant there was no one to stop him from kissing her. Because, ever since she'd walked into his office Tuesday morning, he'd been thinking almost nonstop about just that—kissing Harley Welsh.

He knew it was a bad idea—but it didn't stop him from thinking about it. A lot. While he was grappling with what to do next, Harley bolted.

With a, "Right," and a hasty, "Good night," she grabbed her bag, and after all but running down the hall, slipped out the front door.

Josh ran a hand along the back of his neck and stared at the closed door for a solid five minutes, contemplating her hasty exit. Was she running from him? From herself? Was she as confused as he was over what was happening between them? With a sigh, he headed into the kitchen for a glass of water. There, on the counter, was a handwritten copy of the Welshes' Pumpkin Patch Fall Festival Countdown. She'd left a copy of the checklist for him. And changed Welsh to McBride. Number one, pumpkin carving, had been checked.

He scanned the page, spotted a small starred note at the bottom of the page. A note and a phone number written below it. He read it once, then again and smiled. Harley's hand writing was looped and happy—very Harley. He stuck the note to his fridge. That way he wouldn't lose her phone number.

The stew was good. I think you can carve the rest of the pumpkins on your own. Just in case, here is my number. – Harley

Chapter Six

HARLEY CHECKED HER phone before tucking it into the pocket of her purse. It was only pathetic to keep checking her phone if someone knew she was doing it, right? And no one knew…she hoped. Autumn had been surprised when she announced she was going to the football game, but she'd happily offered to come with her.

"I am starving," Autumn said. "Like haven't-eaten-in-a-week starving."

Harley laughed. "Or six hours ago."

"But, really, does a salad count?"

"I think so. It's food." Harley sipped her water.

"Well, it's not very filling." Autumn checked her phone and smiled. "Noah is on his way. And he'll buy us popcorn."

"Good. Want to go to the Main Street Café after the game?" Harley asked. "Get a milkshake?"

"Deal." Autumn nodded. "I'm assuming we're here for Nadia? Is she going to sit with us?"

"I don't know." On Thursday, she'd promised Nadia she would come to the game. But she hadn't heard a thing from Josh since Wednesday night—when she'd panicked and run out of his place instead of launching herself at him. She'd wanted to. She'd thought about it. Being wrapped up in his redwood-tree-sized arms and—

"What's up?" Autumn asked.

"Nothing." Harley pretended to look for something in her bag in a pathetic attempt to dodge her sister's question.

"Uh-huh." Autumn exhaled slowly. "So, you know how you were all over me about Noah and how cute he was and how I totally had a thing for him?" She paused but Harley didn't respond. "And I was all, no I don't. Then you gave me that look—you know the one. The 'Whatever' look. Well, it's my turn. I get that Coach McBride isn't as communicative or funny or cute as Noah but you two totally have something going on."

"Something? Yes, we do have—"

"Ha!" Autumn clapped her hands together. "I so knew it."

Harley grabbed her hand. "Nadia. Trying to give a little girl some fun is what's going on." She lowered her voice. "That's it."

"Right. Let me know when you come around." She leaned forward. "Because, from what I've seen, you two have some serious chemistry. I'm surprised the two of you didn't make a few pumpkins spontaneously combust out at Krieger Farms."

Harley had to laugh then. Hard.

"Miss Harley?" Nadia was on the sideline. "See, Daddy,

she's here."

Harley stood and waved, carefully stepping over the rest of the row and heading down the steps. She leaned over the bar separating the bleachers from the sideline. "I promised. I like your purple-and-gold shirt."

"Mrs. Reed made it for me." Nadia stretched her shirtfront and pointed at the design. "The Wild Cat paw print."

"Harley." Josh was calm and brusque. "Mrs. Reed did offer to come so you don't have to watch Nadia—"

"Not to burst your bubble, Coach, but Nadia is the reason I'm here. She's part of my cheer squad now." Harley shrugged. "I brought pom-poms and everything."

"Pom-poms?" Nadia was hopping with excitement.

Josh chuckled.

Josh chuckling. Danger zone. Not looking.

She winked at Nadia and ignored the slight jump in her pulse. "Does that mean she can sit with me? Tucker too? Since I have pom-poms and I'm pretty sure Mrs. Reed doesn't."

"Tucker's at a sleepover with friends. Let me touch base with Mrs. Reed." Josh was still chuckling. "Hopefully she isn't on her way."

"I guess I should have called." Harley risked looking his way. *Yep.* He was as big and handsome as ever. She cleared her throat, shoving Autumn's 'serious chemistry' comment aside. "To confirm," she added. Not that she had his phone number... Even though she'd left hers for him.

Josh didn't respond, his fingers typing out something on his phone. He nodded then. "Okay. Have fun. Going up." He lifted Nadia up high enough for Harley to reach her. "Cheer loud, Nadia. The team likes it."

Harley smiled, lifting Nadia over the bar and holding her close. "The louder the better," she whispered. "So, so loud. Right?"

Nadia giggled. "Right."

Harley was proud of herself for making it back to her seat without looking back or making a fool of herself by ogling Coach McBride before half of Crossvine Creek. Even Autumn couldn't say a thing over how normal that interaction had been. Perfectly normal. Now she could sit back and relax and enjoy cheering with Nadia—without getting ridiculously googly-eyed over Josh.

At least, that was the plan. But her sister was watching her with wide eyes and Noah was staring awfully hard at their popcorn, laughing.

"What?" Harley asked, setting Nadia on the seat between them. "Is everything okay?"

"Um…" Autumn said. "Yes."

"Noah?" Harley asked, leaning forward.

"All good." Noah gave her a thumbs-up, still chuckling. "Want some popcorn Nadia?"

Harley did a quick sweep of the stands, looking for a possible explanation for Autumn's out-of-character expression and silence. Of the two of them, Autumn was the talker. Big-time. Sometimes, too much. Before the night was over, she'd hear all about whatever her sister was overanalyzing.

"Pom-poms." Harley put her large canvas bag in her lap and pulled out the three sets of small pom-poms—all in gold and purple.

"I don't get any?" Noah asked, laughing.

"We can share." Autumn handed him the purple pom-pom.

"What if I wanted gold?" He nudged her.

Autumn traded pom-poms.

"Nah, I think I'd rather have purple." He smirked.

Nadia laughed.

"He is funny, isn't he?" Harley asked.

"He thinks so." Autumn smiled, leaning into Noah as he draped his arm around her.

"One of the many reasons you love me." Noah kissed her cheek.

The pom-poms were a hit. Unlike last time, it didn't take Nadia long to embrace her inner cheerleader. By halftime, one of the high school cheerleaders had invited the little girl down onto the field.

"Will you come with me?" Nadia asked.

Harley took her hand and led Nadia down the steps, to the end of the bleachers, and down the last set of steps that led to the field.

"Hi, Miss Harley. Nadia, right?" one of the girls asked. "I'm Ashley. You are an awesome cheerleader."

"I like your pom-poms," another girl said. "I'm Ramona. But you can call me Mona. And this is Rebecca." She pointed at the final cheerleader, who waved.

"We were talking and thought you might want to come to a cheer practice next week. We have a junior cheer club going," Ashley said.

Nadia's grip tightened on Harley's hand but at least she wasn't hiding.

Harley winked at her. "Cheer club sounds like a lot of fun."

"We even have uniforms," Mona added. "You get to cheer at the Thanksgiving game with us. And ride on the Christmas float. There's only three of us, so we always like help."

"All you have to do is cheer and clap and wave those pom-poms." Rebecca shook her pom-poms.

Nadia finally spoke. "Miss Harley got them for me."

Ashley nodded. "Miss Harley is awesome."

"That's nice to hear." Harley hugged her former student. "You know, Nadia, I think you should give cheer club a try."

"My little sister is in it, too," Ashley said, pointing into the stands.

Harley waved at the little girl in the stands. "You know, Katie, don't you, Nadia?"

Katie wore face paint, was shaking pom-poms, and wearing a smaller version of the cheerleaders' uniform. She was one of those kids who constantly needed something to do.

She was busy and precocious and outgoing—and just the sort of friend Nadia needed.

Nadia swallowed, nervous. "She's in my class."

"That's great." Ashley smiled. "You already have a friend, then."

Nadia gazed into the bleachers, hesitating briefly before returning Katie's wave.

"Can you talk to Coach about it, Miss Harley?" Mona asked, leaning closer. "He's sort of...intimidating."

"Yeah, way intimidating." Ashley shrugged. "I really think Nadia would have fun."

"I'll talk to him," Harley said. The team was heading back onto the field, with Josh bringing up the rear. When he saw them, he headed their way clipboard in hand.

"Oh." Ashley stepped back. "We've got to get back to it."

"Nice to meet you, Nadia," Rebecca said.

"See you this week," Mona added.

"Bye." Nadia waved.

"Everything okay?" Josh asked, brow furrowed.

"Everything is great. Nadia has just been invited to join the junior cheerleading club." She was still holding Nadia's hand so she gave her arm a wiggle. "Pretty exciting stuff."

"Cheerleading club, huh?" Josh knelt. "Well, now. That sounds like fun."

Nadia nodded.

"You want to be a junior cheerleader?" he asked.

Nadia nodded again.

"Cheerleader club and art lessons, huh? Sounds like you're going to be busy." Josh glanced up at her.

What was it about him that shifted her heart rate into high gear? *Focus.* Not on Josh. On cheer club. "One of her classmates is in the club too—Katie. She's a ball of energy," Harley added, watching one of his slow smiles take shape. A man shouldn't be this good-looking. It wasn't fair. "We should get back. You have a game to coach."

He stood, but his gaze never left her face. What was he waiting for? Or, was he looking for something? He had to be able to hear her heart. Had to feel the ripple between them. Was that why he was staring?

"If… If you're free afterward, Autumn, Noah and I are going to get something to eat at Main Street Café. We need to firm up plans for the Farmer's Market." *Why am I inviting him to join us?* Her invitation went against the whole keeping-distance thing. "But…I guess it will be too late so—"

"It's a Friday night," Josh said. "I… Well…" He was suddenly mesmerized by his clipboard. "Gotta go." He ruffled Nadia's hair. "Keep up the good work."

"I will, Daddy." Nadia skip-hopped her way back to the stands and all the way back to their seats.

While Noah shared a new bag of popcorn, Harley dug through her purse for some lip balm. It wasn't as cold as the last game, but her lips were dry all the same. That's when she realized her phone was vibrating.

She read the text. Grabbing a bite to eat sounds good.

The Farmer's Market is number two on the list. I checked. Looking forward to it.

She smiled. He'd read the copy she left him.

Another text pinged. This is Josh. And this is my number.

She laughed. The game was in full swing so texting him didn't make much sense. Besides, they'd have plenty of opportunity to work out the details after the game. It would be fine. Autumn and Noah would be there to keep things from getting too stilted between them.

She and Nadia cheered and clapped and had a great time but Harley found her attention wandering to Josh again and again. Maybe she wasn't up to this joint checklist adventure. It wasn't because she didn't want to spend time with Nadia and do everything she could to help the little girl make friends and find her place in her new hometown. No, that was all well and good.

Harley's dilemma was one hundred percent about Josh McBride. What exactly was she supposed to do about the bottomless well of thoughts and feelings and longing he stirred? And how was she supposed to keep her distance when she was beginning to realize that staying away was the last thing she wanted to do?

JOSH HAD PICKED up dinner from Main Street Café on more

than one occasion since they'd moved to Crossvine Creek. It had regular business—a fixture on the town's Main Street—but he'd never seen it like this.

"This is still the place to be after a football game. It was just like this when I was a Crossvine Creek Wild Cat," Noah explained, sliding around the booth to make room for him and Nadia. "Guess some things never change. Next week it will be even crazier, since it's homecoming."

"The amazing milkshakes help." Autumn nodded. "I recommend the chocolate, by the way."

"Autumn loves chocolate," Harley added. "I'm more a vanilla girl myself. Or, if I'm feeling adventurous, strawberry. Which do you like?"

While Harley was reading the menu to Nadia, Josh was inundated with handshakes and congratulations. Most of the football team was there—as well as all their parents—and everyone was pretty upbeat about their continued winning streak.

"Your daddy is a regular hometown celebrity," Autumn said to Nadia.

"He's the coach. It's a big job," Harley explained. "Bringing a team together is hard work."

He hadn't expected a compliment from Harley, but it felt good to get one. Even better when she smiled at him. She had a beautiful smile. *This is going well.*

Thankfully, the food arrived and the focus shifted. Nadia was all smiles when her chicken strips and strawberry milkshake were delivered. She was halfway through her food when Ashley, the cheerleader, came to the table—a little girl in tow.

"Coach, it was a great game tonight. All the players think you're the best coach ever."

"There was definitely plenty to cheer about, wasn't there, Ashley?" Harley asked.

"Yes, ma'am," Ashley agreed. "We didn't want to interrupt your dinner. Katie just wanted to say 'hi' real quick."

Josh was impressed by the confidence that rolled off of little Katie. She climbed up next to Nadia in the booth. "Is that strawberry?" Katie asked, waiting until Nadia nodded to go on. "It's good. I like grilled cheese. And French fries."

He watched, curious to see how his quiet little girl would react.

"Want one?" Nadia asked, offering the other girl a fry.

"Okay." Katie took the French fry. "Are you in cheer? You get to dress like me. We wear glitter on our face sometimes, too. And sometimes face paint." She paused long enough to finish off the fry. "We always get to yell and jump up and down."

Nadia inspected Katie's uniform with a look Josh knew all too well. It was the same look she wore when she saw a dog. He bit back a sigh—but Harley noticed. With a slight shrug, she looked between Katie and Nadia then back at him, her smile hopeful.

He understood. Nadia needed a friend. This was a good

thing. A very good thing.

"See." Katie pointed at the sparkles sewn onto her top. "Cheerleaders don't get the sparkles."

"Let her think about it, Katie." Ashley smiled.

"Okay," Katie sighed, taking another French fry. "But you should do it." She slipped from the booth. "See you later, alligator."

Nadia gave a shy smile.

"Now you say: after a while, crocodile," Katie said, taking hold of her sister's hand.

"After a while, crocodile." Nadia giggled.

Katie giggled too, waving as they walked across the restaurant to several tables clustered together. The football players, cheerleaders, and—from the looks of it—every teen in Crossvine Creek were enjoying their victory.

"She's funny," Nadia said.

"Yes," Harley agreed. "She is."

"Is she in your class?" Josh asked.

"Yes." Nadia shrugged. "She's got lots and lots of friends."

"And she wants you to be one of them." Harley paused, then added, "I did like the sparkles on her uniform."

Nadia yawned. "Me too."

"Well, I guess we should jump right in, before Nadia falls asleep on us." Harley laughed, pulling the folded paper from her purse. "Tomorrow is the Farmer's Market. We can meet there around ten...if that's not too early?"

"Nope." It didn't matter what day of the week it was, he was up with sun.

"Wear something you can get wet," Harley added, scanning the list.

"What?" he asked, looking at Noah for clarification.

"Bobbing for apples," Noah confirmed.

"And don't forget about the scarecrow contest." Autumn leaned against Noah. "That's always fun. They sell the scarecrows to raise money for the animal shelter."

It wasn't the first time Josh was struck by how different his life had been a year ago. Bobbing for apples, scarecrow making, and holiday yard decorations? Different wasn't quite the right word. Dallas had had its fair share of things to do, but Lolly had been the one who'd chauffeured the kids around. He'd missed so much. *Not anymore.*

"You're already decorated for Halloween this week—I'll be handing out candy so you and the kids better stop by that night." Her finger tapped the list. "We always plan our family fall art class right about the time the kids are all over their Halloween sugar high. This year, our fall art class is next Monday and we're making clove apples." Harley paused. "Sound good?"

But he'd gotten hung up on Halloween... Lolly had been a Halloween pro. The costumes. And candy. Trick-or-treating. Considering everything Harley and her family were already doing for his kids, he'd have to figure out Halloween on his own. Or he could ask Mrs. Reed for help.

"Josh?" Harley asked, watching him. "Have your kids ever made clove apples?"

"Um, no?" He had no idea what a clove apple was.

"Well you're missing out so plan to be there," Harley said, shaking her head. "Are you free?"

"Next Monday." He sipped his iced tea. "Yes, we're free."

"Also, Nadia said she wanted me to make dinner. I thought I'd bring over everything to make apple dumplings together. We can take them to the Fall Festival as prizes for the cakewalk." She paused. "Does Wednesday night sound okay?"

"My calendar is wide open." Carefully, he pulled Nadia close—using his leg for her pillow. "Except for Friday night. It's game night. And this Friday is homecoming."

"Homecoming." Harley glanced at Nadia. "She will love that."

"Will this be a regular thing now?" Autumn asked. "Game night?"

That caught Josh's attention. "You don't normally go to the games?"

He caught the color staining Harley's cheeks as she bent lower, over her checklist.

"Normally only the one." Autumn Welsh was smiling like she had a secret.

"I don't mind," Noah said. "Especially the way we're playing."

Harley's words came out in a rush. "But if Mrs. Reed is counting on the income—"

"She's not," Josh interrupted. He liked having Harley in the stands. Was that a bad thing? "Still, I'm sure there are other things you need to do." Up until now, they'd seemed to have some sort of silent understanding to be on their best behavior. Quick looks only—if at all—and sitting on opposite sides of the table. That way, there could be no worries about a public awkward display. Granted, he'd spent more time than he should watching Harley with Nadia in the stands—something Autumn Welsh had obviously noticed.

Now that he and Harley had made eye contact, there was a tangible shift in the air. He couldn't help but notice just how amazing her eyes were. A mix of gold and chocolate. Warm. If he had to pick a word for Harley, it would be warm. That was who she was. Warm and inviting, welcoming and kind... "I don't want to take advantage of your kindness." His voice was a little gruff but, hopefully, not noticeably so.

"I told you—everything on this list is a family tradition." Harley glanced around the table. "We'd be doing it without you, so we might as well do it with you all. Isn't that right, Autumn?"

"Well, yes. The football isn't on the list, of course, but everything else? Definitely." Autumn nodded. "And the Fall Festival is so much fun."

"The pie-eating contest," Noah said, pointing at himself. "Last year's champion."

"What kind of pie?" Josh asked.

"Mostly apple and pumpkin." Noah's eyes narrowed. "But I'm just letting you know—don't get any ideas. You can't beat me."

Josh laughed.

"And then there are hay rides and the corn-row maze opens." Harley's excitement was tangible. "Fall is really and truly here."

A full month of fall activities—of pumpkins and scarecrows and hay rides and whatever else Harley had jotted down on the list he'd stuck to the refrigerator door. Not *even* a full month—twenty-seven days. He could manage twenty-seven days. He hoped.

"Will you be staying here for the holidays?" Autumn asked. "Or going to visit family?"

"It's just me and the kids." He ran his hand over Nadia's curls. "I should probably get her home. Sounds like tomorrow is going to be a busy day." He scooped Nadia up. "Thanks for including us." He liked Noah—liked the Welshes. His daughter wasn't the only one who needed friends.

"Sure." Harley stood. "I'll get the door."

He should argue with her but he didn't.

"See you tomorrow," Noah said.

Josh followed Harley to the door, smiling and nodding

as the parents, players, and restaurant patrons wished him a good evening and offered more congratulations over tonight's win.

"It's gotten colder." Harley held the door wide, then followed him out.

"You don't have your coat." He frowned.

"I'm fine." She trailed after him to the Jeep. "Josh, can I ask you something?"

He opened the Jeep and buckled Nadia into her car seat—she didn't stir. Once the door was closed, he turned. Something about her tone made him hesitate. "Yes."

"Who's Lolly?" Harley paused. "Nadia has mentioned her on more than one occasion." She hurried on. "You can tell me this is none of my business—I can take it."

She was right, it wasn't any of her business. But he found himself telling her anyway. "Lolly was my mother. My wife died when Nadia was a few months old so Lolly moved in and pretty much ran the house and raised the kids… But she passed about eight months ago." He drew in a deep breath and the words kept coming. "Nadia was with her, in the grocery store, like they'd done a hundred times. Mom had a stroke." He shook his head. "It took me a while to get to Nadia…" He cleared his throat. "I'm pretty sure that's why she's so shy and panics in crowds."

Harley was sliding her arms around his waist before he realized it. "I'm so, so sorry, Josh." Her words were muffled against his chest. "Truly."

Without thought, he wrapped his arms around her. It felt good. *She* felt good.

"About your wife and your mother." Her hands pressed against his back. "I know how devastating it is to lose your mother. It's a horrible thing."

His nose rested against her temple, in no hurry to let her go. Other than the wind, the muffled chatter of conversations taking place inside the café, and the occasional car passing by, it was silent. And he didn't mind. He closed his eyes, closed out the world, and concentrated on the comfort she gave.

"Is that why you moved here?" she murmured.

"We needed a fresh start—someplace where I could put the kids first. Someplace where no one was a stranger." Clearly, he hadn't put enough thought into that part.

"You picked the right place." There was a smile in her voice.

"I don't know. Sometimes I think it was too much change, too fast." He'd never said as much out loud.

"I can only imagine how difficult this has been—for all of you." Harley pulled back to look up at him. "Nadia will be okay… You're making sure of that."

He was trying. "I'm sorry about your mother."

"Thank you." She rested a hand against his chest.

He covered her hand with his. "Your fingers are frozen." *Because she's standing outside without a coat on.*

"I'm fine," she argued, a breathless quality to her words.

What am I doing?

He had to stop this—had to stop putting himself in this situation. If he didn't, he'd kiss her. He was pretty sure she wanted him to. He knew he wanted to…

It couldn't happen. He was in no shape to pursue a relationship with anyone. He didn't want a romantic relationship—or anything else that would distract him from what mattered—his kids. The combination of sheer loneliness and the intense attraction he had for Harley was a recipe for disaster. But unlike losing his mother—and Bethany before that—he could control this.

He had to.

Starting now.

There'd be no more touching. No more moments alone. No more situations that would make him want all the things he shouldn't have. No more mixed signals. "Harley." He swallowed. "I want us to be clear." He swallowed again. "About what…this…what we're doing here."

She nodded, looking almost hopeful. "I think that's a good idea."

"I appreciate your help. My kids and I need kindness. Especially Nadia. You've given that to us all. And I'm grateful." He paused, slowly stepping away—putting space between them. "I wanted to let you know that, beyond friendship, I have nothing to give. I wanted to make sure we were on the same page."

Harley blinked, her gaze falling from his. "You mean,

between you and me?" She sounded confused. "*No.* Of course not. I'm not... You thought... No. We would *never* work." She pointed back and forth between them.

Never work. She sounded so confident—almost in shock that he'd implied differently. He frowned. They had a lot to learn about each other, sure, but never work? Never was an awful strong word... *Hold up.* This was good. This was what he wanted. Did he feel a little foolish for reading more into this? Yes. But he'd been out of commission for so long, it wasn't really his fault, was it? He was wrong. She wasn't interested. "Okay." So why didn't he feel okay about this?

"Besides, you have kids..." She shook her head. "No. I don't want...you and me?" She cleared her throat. "No. The hug? Sorry. It's just you lost your mom and I lost mine..."

The more she talked, the more ridiculous he felt. The bite to the air seemed sharper now. Colder.

"This is about Nadia." She took a deep breath. "We'll get through the checklist and junior cheer camp and then I'll be out of your hair in no time."

Good. "Okay," he practically growled.

"I'll see you in the morning at the Farmer's Market, then." Her laugh sounded off. "Hugs for Nadia only from now on—I promise. Glad we cleared that up." She drew in a deep breath. "Good night, then."

"Night," he grumbled, waiting until she was inside before he climbed into the Jeep, his hands tightening around the steering wheel. He should be happy. She had no interest in him—none. He groaned, remembering the way she'd practically run from his house—how she'd tried to back out of his office. She'd been trying to *avoid* being alone with him. How had he misread that so completely? *Great.* He'd made a total fool out of himself. He should be happy she hadn't called off their agreement right there.

He put the Jeep in gear, backed out, and headed home.

You have kids. She'd been shaking her head. Then said something else. She didn't want, *what?* Kids? He hadn't expected that. Harley was so good with Nadia and the other students… But that was different than being a mother.

Still, it helped to know how she felt. He and the kids were a package deal. When he was ready to date again, if that ever happened, he'd make sure to pick a woman who wanted the whole package—period. Apparently, that wasn't Harley Welsh.

Chapter Seven

"GOOD MORNING." HARLEY waved as she walked past Dickinson's pecan decorated-canopy topped booth. The scent of cinnamon and caramel wafted from the old-fashioned roaster Mr. Dickinson would spin occasionally, keeping the candied pecans from sticking or scorching.

"Morning," Mrs. Dickinson called back, handing her a small plastic cup with a sample. "We added maple this year. What do you think?"

Harley took the sample cup. "It certainly smells delicious." She popped one of the still-warm nuts into her mouth. "Oh, yum. This is like tasting fall." She bought two bags—one maple and one classic candied—and wandered to the next booth.

She loved the Farmer's Market. Loved seeing all the small businesses from neighboring communities, loved the smiles and friendly faces—and the wide array of treats. But this morning, she was struggling.

"I got you one." Autumn handed her a small to-go coffee cup. "What is that heavenly smell?"

Harley passed her the pecans and hooked arms with her

sister. "It's a pretty perfect morning, don't you think?"

"It would be—if you were smiling." Autumn looked her way. "And don't try to feed me the 'I'm just tired' excuse you used on Dad. There is way more to it than that."

Harley avoided eye contact. "Whatever. How about we enjoy this crisp, clear and sunny morning."

Autumn raised an eyebrow. "Don't *whatever* me. You know you can't keep secrets from me so why bother trying?"

"I just love all the delicious smells," Harley continued as if her sister hadn't said a thing. "I have a feeling I'm going to be buying a lot of goodies."

Autumn made a production out of searching the crowd. "Where is your hunky coach? I mean, where is Nadia?"

Harley swallowed down her sigh and took a sip of coffee. *Where indeed?*

After last night, she wondered if they'd show up today. Then again, he wasn't the one who had been thoroughly humiliated. Had she been staring up at him hoping he'd, maybe, kiss her? Yes. Instead he'd gently disentangled himself and proceeded to explain he was not interested in her—just the help she'd offered with Nadia. He'd been kind, but firm. He'd made it clear he still wanted her help—just not *her*.

It had hurt. It *did* hurt. She hadn't been expecting that.

"Are they coming?" Autumn asked.

"I think so." She popped another candied pecan into her mouth and feigned interest in a hand-stitched Thanksgiving table runner hanging from the closest booth.

Hurt or not, this wasn't about her. She wasn't spending time with Josh and his children to spend time with *him*.

Now that she knew the extent of loss Josh and his family had been through, she understood the connection they shared.

And Nadia? Seeing her Lolly collapse? Being surrounded by strangers, scared and alone? Poor little girl. Harley's heart ached just thinking about it. For Josh too—it was clear he felt guilty about it. Not that there was a thing he could have done to prevent what had happened. Still…she was his little girl. She came first—Tucker too.

Hurt aside, Harley respected his dedication to his children.

Now that she knew where she stood with Josh, there would be no more casual touches or lingering stares or ridiculous butterflies or stirrings or…any of it. From here on out, she was the McBride family's very own Mary Poppins. She even had the giant purse to prove it.

"What are you thinking, right now?" Autumn asked.

"About Mary Poppins." Harley paused, scanning the Bob for Apples sign-up sheet. "Should I sign us up?"

"I am not bobbing for apples." Autumn shook her head. "Are we, Cobie? Well, on second thought, Cobie might."

Cobie stared up at her, tail wagging and ears perked.

"I'm pretty sure this is a humans-only sort of competition." Harley smiled.

"Don't listen to your auntie Harley, Cobie." Autumn crouched, rubbing her black Lab behind the ear. "She just knows you'd win, that's all."

"What about Noah?" Harley asked.

"Oh, definitely sign him up." Autumn laughed.

"Sign who up? And for what?" Their father joined them. "You're looking awfully mischievous, Autumn."

"Not to worry, Dad. You're safe…this time." Autumn stood and winked his way.

"Poor Noah." Their father sighed.

Autumn laughed. "Have you seen my *poor* Noah?"

"I saw his truck circling the park as I was walking this way." Their father shook his head. "Not that much parking. Looks like a really good turnout."

"Miss Harley!" Even over the lull of voices, laughter, and general commotion of the milling crowd, Harley heard Nadia's sweet voice. "Miss Harley!"

Harley turned right as Nadia attached herself to her calves, hugging tightly. "Good morning, Nadia." She reached down to pat the little girl's back. "Don't you look ready for fall." Nadia's long-sleeved brown dress was covered in tiny embroidered leaves. "I think I like this dress almost as much as I liked your pumpkin one."

Nadia was all smiles. "I dressed myself. Daddy did my braids." Her braids were crooked and her tights looked like they were inside out, but she looked one hundred percent adorable.

129

"I *tried* to do her braids." Josh's voice was low and gruff and, when Harley looked up, she saw his almost apologetic shrug.

Harley was proud of her lack of lingering or noticing how his navy sweater made his chest even more wall-like than usual and his blue eyes super bright… *Great work.*

"Braiding takes time." Their father clapped Josh on the shoulder. "I gave up. But I can do a ponytail, one-handed."

"That's true, he can." Harley smiled, taking Nadia's hand. "I think this is an admirable attempt at braids, Josh— you should keep at it." She did not even risk a look at him. "I think we should start at O'Hanlons' booth, Nadia. They have goats."

"Real live goats?" Nadia's eyes went round.

"Real live." Harley nodded.

"Can you touch them?" Tucker asked. "Do they bite?"

"I have never been bitten by a goat." Harley shrugged. "But, just to be sure, we'd better ask Mr. O'Hanlon."

"Wait." Autumn held up the clipboard. "You should sign up, Coach McBride."

Josh took the clipboard. "Bobbing for apples?" One brow rose. "Um…"

"It's all in good fun," Autumn told him. "Noah is pretty good at it though so—"

"I'm good at what?" Noah asked as soon as he'd joined the group.

"Bobbing for apples," Autumn said, leaning into his hug.

"Oh." Noah frowned. "Pie-eating competition yes. Bobbing for apples? Not a fan. Germs."

"Like an oversized petri dish." Harley wrinkled her nose. "Lovely. I hadn't thought of it that way. Guess I'll be taking that one off the list."

"What's bobbing for apples?" Tucker asked.

While her father, Josh, and Noah explained the particulars of the contest, Nadia's attention wandered around the crowd. Her little hand tightened on Harley's, so tight, that Harley crouched by her side and asked, "What's up, Nadia?"

Nadia didn't say a word. Instead, she pointed—at a booth at the end of the row of tents and tables.

"That's the animal shelter booth." Harley glanced in the direction Nadia pointed.

Nadia kept on pointing. Not at the booth, but at a dog. A black-and-white dog who was resting its paws on the top of the pen—staring their way. "So pretty."

"It is," Harley agreed, daring a look at Josh.

He was frowning, his own gaze locked on the dog that had so captured his daughter's attention.

Harley felt for him, she did. Watching as he ran a hand over his face, took a deep breath, and set his jaw, she couldn't help but wonder what was going on inside that gorgeous head of his... *Nice.* It was true. He *was* gorgeous. She might as well accept that as a fact. *He is a gorgeous devoted father who is not interested in me.* It stung, but it snapped her out of it.

"I guess we're headed that way." Josh's glance her way was quick, the tick in his jaw muscle fleeting.

Sympathy rose up, making her say, "The goats are super cool, Nadia. You can feed them."

"Unless they bite." Tucker clearly wasn't sold on the whole goat thing.

"No." Noah shook his head. "Goats don't bite."

"The goats will wait." Josh held out his hand to his daughter. "Let's go check that last booth out." Tucker took his other hand.

"Do they want a dog?" Her father's question was a whisper.

"I don't think Josh does," she answered.

"I hate to break it to him but he'll be leaving with one." Her father smiled, squeezing her shoulder. "Especially once Cynthia gets a hold of them."

It was true. Her father's girlfriend, Cynthia Contreras, wasn't just an animal advocate or animal shelter volunteer; she had an uncanny ability to help animals and people come together. And, right now, Josh and his kids were heading straight for her. While Autumn led Noah and their father back to the Dickinsons' booth, Harley followed Josh and the kids. The closer they got to the black and white dog, the harder the dog's tail wagged.

She wasn't sure who was more excited: the dog or Tucker and Nadia. Barely suppressed excitement rolled off all three of them.

Josh glanced her way, his smile reluctant.

His smile. As always, it set off a chain of tingles and shudders that, sadly, hadn't been the least bit dampened by Josh's friends-only proclamation.

"Good morning, Coach," Cynthia said when she caught sight of them. "And good morning to you two, as well. We've got some precious fur babies looking for their forever home. Are you looking for a dog or a cat or—"

"That one." Nadia pointed at the black and white dog who was attempting to scale the enclosure.

"Oh," Cynthia chuckled. "It looks like Chewie sees you too."

"Chewie?" Josh practically groaned.

"Because he's fluffy like that shaggy character in that science-fiction movie? Chewie? Or something." Cynthia was still smiling.

"Not because he chews on things?" Josh asked.

"No." Cynthia shook her head. "No more than the average dog."

"I'm not sure what that means." He glanced at Cynthia, then the dog, then at Harley.

Harley shrugged. "Don't look at me. Autumn's the dog owner."

"Daddy." Nadia tugged her father's hand. "Come on. Let's meet him."

"Yeah, Dad." Tucker tugged the other hand. "Give him a chance."

"You can take him into the dog park, if you like," Cynthia suggested. "He loves to play fetch."

"Please, Daddy. You told me to try new things." Nadia stared up at her father. "Try real hard, even if you don't want to."

"I did say that." Josh's expression was equal parts adoration and defeat.

"You said you have to take risks," Tucker added. "Big risks lead to big rewards, I remember."

"Of course, you do. Now." Josh chuckled. "Remember, I was talking about trying out for the soccer team."

"Dad." Tucker shook his head. "Tell him, Miss Harley."

Harley hugged herself, aware that three pair of bright blue eyes were waiting for her to say something. She was torn. Did she side with Josh and try to dampen the kids' enthusiasm over Chewie? *Is that possible?* Or did she side with the kids and plead their case? Then again, she was here for Nadia. *What would Mary Poppins do?* "One game of fetch can't harm anything, can it?" She shrugged. "How risky can it be?"

"THAT'S IT?" JOSH asked, handing the adoption paperwork to Cynthia Contreras.

"Relatively painless," she said, smiling.

"I'm going to hold you to that." He was kidding. Sort of.

One look at his kids had told him he'd be taking the dog home. After the first game of fetch, he'd managed to get them to explore a little more. The scarecrow *race* was the high point of the morning. Watching Harley, Autumn, and Noah assemble a handyman scarecrow—Noah's idea, Autumn said—in thirty minutes was a distraction. He hadn't laughed that hard in a long time. In the end, though, he had to admit that their scarecrow was the best. Next year, he'd have to remember to bring some cast-off items so he and the kids could make a football scarecrow.

But once the scarecrows were made and packed away to be sold at the Pumpkin Patch Fall Festival next weekend, Nadia and Tucker had made a beeline back to the animal shelter booth. After another game of fetch, he'd pulled them away long enough to watch the goats get milked, learn how goat cheese was made, and determine whether or not goats did bite. They did not.

But now, Chewie sat at his side, watching every move Josh made. If he hadn't known better, he'd have thought the dog was smiling at him. Dogs didn't smile. Did they?

"He says thank you," Harley offered.

"He does?" Josh shot Harley a look. "You know this because?"

"Look at him." Harley pointed. "He's smiling at you."

"He is, Daddy." Nadia nodded, holding on to Chewie's leash with both hands. "He says thank you. He does."

"You're welcome," he said to the dog.

Chewie stood, his black plume of a tail—tipped with white—swishing in the air. Maybe Chewie was grateful. While Harley and the kids had played fetch with the dog the third and final time, he'd learned all about Chewie's history. Considering how well-trained Chewie was, Josh was curious about how the dog had ended up in the shelter. But his owner, a soldier, had been deployed and there'd been no one able to take Chewie so…

Now Chewie belonged to them.

"I guess we're done here?" Josh asked, scanning the remaining tents and canopies that had made up this morning's bustling Farmer's Market.

Tucker devoured the last of his caramel apple.

Nadia didn't acknowledge his question—she was too in awe of the dog to care about anything else.

"Then let's go," Autumn said. "We can get you set up."

Noah and Autumn had been the levelheaded ones. Levelheaded as in giving him some practical advice on what he'd need for Chewie—not talking him out of adopting a dog. Instead of making a list, they decided a group visit to the local feed and pet-supply shop was in order.

"Are you sure?" Josh asked again. "I don't want you to have to leave if there are still things you want to do. You know, part of your tradition." He couldn't help but glance Harley's way then.

She smiled at him. "No worries."

"Besides, Cobie needs more food," Autumn assured him,

hooking arms with Noah, and setting off.

"You've got him?" Josh asked Nadia.

Nadia nodded.

"He has no interest in taking off," Autumn said. "You might not have figured this part out yet but…Chewie picked you."

No arguing that. The minute that Nadia and the dog had made eye contact, he'd known his fate was sealed.

At least he's trained. Josh watched the dog, tail curled up and swishing like a fan, trotting between his kids as if that was where he'd always belonged.

"How are you holding up?" Harley's face was a mix of sympathy and amusement. A light gust of wind blew her hair forward, so she reached up to push it back.

Josh was proud of his restraint. All day long, he'd made sure not to let his gaze linger over Harley. Not her red sweater or her black skirt. Not how rosy her cheeks were or how bright her smile was. But he'd noticed the dark smudges beneath her eyes. Had she had trouble sleeping last night?

I know the feeling.

He'd left the café knowing he'd done the right thing. But by the time he got home, showered, and went to bed—he felt like a fool all over again. Why had he immediately jumped to the conclusion that she was interested in him? Just because he was interested in her didn't mean she'd automatically reciprocate.

In the end, this was what he wanted. This was the best

for all of them.

They were halfway through the park when someone called out.

"Harley?" The man waved his arm. "Harley Welsh?"

Harley turned, saw the man, and lit up. "Grant?" She hurried toward the man. "When did you get home from New York? How are you?"

Grant gabbed her in a big hug and spun her around. "You look gorgeous as ever."

Harley was laughing.

Josh turned, stooping to double-check the leash was secured to Chewie's collar—so he could get control of what he was feeling. It was like getting a sudden, solid kick to the chest, knocking the air from his lungs. Deflated.

He heard Harley ask, "How long are you home?" and held his breath, waiting for Grant's answer.

"I'm back." From the corner of his eyes, Josh couldn't help but notice Grant was still holding on to her hands. "I graduated. Passed the bar. Dad's not retiring for a while but it's time I started learning the ropes at the Maxwell Family Law Firm."

"I'm sure he's thrilled you're back." Harley shook her head. "It's been forever since I saw you last."

He wasn't going to eavesdrop like a kid. He had a dog to take care of. No point waiting on Harley—Autumn and Noah were the ones who'd offered to help him anyway and they were probably already at the car. "Let's get Chewie to the car," Josh said, smiling up at the kids.

"Okay, Daddy." Nadia gave Chewie a pat. "We will get you toys. Lots of bouncy balls."

"Tennis balls work—right, Dad?" Tucker asked.

"They should," Josh agreed, moving along the sidewalk.

"Where's Harley?" Autumn asked, once they'd reached the street where the cars were parked.

"She is talking to some guy." Tucker frowned.

"I think his name was Grant," Josh offered.

"Grant?" Autumn's eyes went round. "Grant Maxwell? He's back? Oh, that's great. He is the sweetest guy."

All Josh could do was nod. It was obvious Harley liked him—so he couldn't be all bad.

"We're waiting on Harley then?" Noah asked.

"Why don't you ride over with Josh and the kids and I'll bring Harley over in a few minutes?" Autumn offered.

"That works." Josh nodded again. "We're this way." Between Chewie's need to stop and smell every bush and light post and a handful of football fans stopping for a chat, the walk to the Jeep took a little longer than he expected. Luckily, the dog jumped into the Jeep with ease—ears perked up and ready to go. With everyone loaded up, they headed down Main Street.

While Tucker and Nadia chattered away about Chewie—whose room he'd sleep in, what color collar he needed, and how fast the dog could run—Josh didn't have to say much. They parked, unloaded, and began the process of equipping themselves for pet ownership.

Nadia, in true Nadia fashion, took her time considering each and every option.

Josh shot Noah a look.

"I'm in no hurry." Noah chuckled.

"That's good." Josh smiled, holding Chewie's leash while Nadia stared at the wall of collars.

"Now that's a picture." Autumn's voice had them turning. "All four of you, standing there, watching little Nadia pick out a collar."

"It's precious," Harley added, all smiles.

Josh was all too fond of that smile. He swallowed and turned back to his daughter.

"Harley." Nadia waved her over. "Come here."

"Do we get a collar or a harness?" Tucker asked, shoving his hands into the pockets of his jeans.

"I don't think Chewie needs a harness." Noah walked closer to the display.

While Noah and Harley offered up the pros and cons of either option, Josh walked Chewie down the aisle. He was restless. Agitated. Irritated. Not over the dog or shopping or the morning they'd shared. All of that had been good. Better than good.

"Everything okay?" Autumn asked. "I know you had doubts about adopting a dog. I hope you weren't pressured into this."

"It was inevitable." Josh looked down at Chewie, who

was smiling up at him. "He's a good dog. Smart. Well behaved. I lucked out. We're going to get along just fine." He smiled at Autumn.

"Harley said she didn't exactly give you backup." Autumn wrinkled up her nose. "She feels a little bad about that."

"Don't get me wrong, I love my kids, but I wouldn't have adopted a dog if I was against it." He glanced at Harley. "It's fine."

"Sorry we were a little behind. Grant Maxwell is an old friend. From high school." Autumn shook her head. "Harley never thought he'd come back here."

"Where did he go?"

"Well, he went to law school in New York." Autumn smiled. "Harley went to art school in New York so they spent a lot of time together. After a year, she decided it wasn't for her and came back home, but she told me that Grant loved it there. She never dreamed he'd come back to Crossvine Creek. But, seeing as the Maxwell Family Law Firm is the only law office in Crossvine Creek, I sort of suspected he'd come home eventually."

Was this the guy who had broken her heart? She'd been awful happy to see him.

"Viola North mentioned something about New York. And Harley." He knew he was playing with fire here. He didn't know Autumn all that well and he was nosing around in something that was none of his business.

Autumn nodded, no trace of a smile on her face now. "Viola North loves to talk. What did she say, exactly?" Her brown eyes met his.

Brush it aside. Shrug it off. Don't push this line of conversation. He didn't need to know. It was *none* of his business. "She said Harley'd had her heart broken."

"That's an understatement." Autumn paused, choosing her words with care. "It's not my story to tell but I will say this much. Harley left for New York confident and hopeful and ready to take the art world by storm. She came back second-guessing everything—her art, her independence, and her self-worth."

Josh was frowning too. "Because of Grant Maxwell?" He hadn't meant to bark.

Autumn blinked. "No. No. Grant would never do that to Harley. It was some guy she met while she was there." Autumn nibbled on the inside of her lip. "No, Grant is the sort of guy who would help her move on, I think. He sees her, you know? Her value?"

Josh was staring at Harley now, watching the way she chatted and laughed with Nadia—and his heart ached a little. Harley Welsh was nothing but...love and warmth and kindness. It was impossible not to see that—to know that—after spending any time with her.

"I am her sister so I'm a bit biased but, to me, Harley is priceless. If she ever does decide to give love a second chance, I hope it will be with someone who feels exactly the same way I do," Autumn said. "I think Grant would."

He swallowed, the image of Harley spinning in Grant Maxwell's arms sending his stomach into knots. Which was ridiculous. What? He didn't want her to be happy? He'd never considered himself a selfish man but now, he wasn't so sure. He didn't want her, but he didn't want anyone else to have her. Was that it?

No. He wanted her. He cared about her. He did. Despite his best efforts, a little more every day…

Because I am a fool.

He could pine after her all he wanted, but it wouldn't change the most important fact: she had no interest in him. *None.* The sooner his heart caught on to that fact, the better.

Chapter Eight

HARLEY AND AUTUMN held an open house every year. It was a time for families to come into the studio, make something for the holidays, and leave all the mess behind.

"Apples?" Autumn asked, placing spools of ribbon on the table.

"Check." Harley eyed the baskets of red apples on each table. "Cloves. I hope we have enough." She winked at her sister.

"I hope we have enough shelf space to store the leftover boxes." Autumn shrugged.

"It was nice of the store to donate them—one less thing we have to pay for." Harley nudged her sister. Financially, they were solid but they always appreciated a donation or a sponsorship. Even if it was two cases of whole cloves.

"I think it was smart to cut the cinnamon pinecones this year." Autumn cut strands of orange, rust, sienna, yellow, and red ribbons for the apple stems. "We'd never have time to finish both projects."

"And we can change the cinnamon pinecones up a little.

Add red and green and silver glitter and make it a Christmas craft." Harley placed a stack of ribbons on each of the work tables.

"Genius." Autumn paused, smiling up from her scissor work.

"Skewers, cloves, apples, ribbons, and glue." Harley glanced at the clock. "We're ready." With a few minutes to spare.

"It was nice to see Grant." Autumn continued to snip ribbon.

"It was." Harley nodded. "I'm honestly surprised he came home though. He just sort of *fit* in New York. He didn't stick out." They'd meet for lunch or dinner to catch up. Grant had always known how to make her laugh. He'd also been the one to introduce her to Oliver—an up-and-coming young lawyer who'd acted as Grant's mentor. Grant had apologized for weeks after their breakup, feeling responsible for Harley's heartbreak—which was ridiculous and she told him so. If anything, she owed Grant. Everything that had happened—her move, meeting Oliver, their engagement, and their breakup—had helped her understand what she really wanted in life. Now that she had it, she wouldn't change a thing; heartbreak or not.

"Maybe, like you, he chose to come back because this is where his heart is," Autumn suggested.

"His dad *has* always been his hero," Harley said. "Honestly, Grant is the kind of guy who can fit in anywhere. And he does seem happy to be home. I do feel for him though. Viola North was descending on him when we left the park."

"I noticed." Autumn giggled. "By now, she'll have a list of women to start throwing his way." She glanced at her sister. "Don't be surprised if you're on that list."

"Please." Harley waved her aside.

"What's wrong with Grant?" Autumn asked, scissors and ribbons forgotten.

"There's nothing wrong with him." *He's not Josh.* "But we're friends. We've always been friends. Since grade school. I remember him eating a box of crayons to see if they tasted the way he imagined colors would taste." She shook her head, laughing.

"Okay, crayon eating aside, some people might think the two of you have potential for the best more-than-friends relationship ever." Autumn started packing her supplies away. "Unless there is someone else you've got your eye on?"

Harley shot her a look—hoping her sister would stop there.

"He was not happy over your little reunion in the park." Autumn crossed the room, pulled her work apron from the peg and tied it on.

Josh hadn't stuck around for her to introduce him to Grant. But that didn't mean he was upset over… *Stop.* He wouldn't be upset. He wouldn't care. There was only one way to end her sister's campaign for a Josh-and-Harley match. "Autumn, Josh told me he doesn't think of me that way."

"What?" Autumn almost dropped her water bottle. "When? Why didn't you tell me? What did he say? Are you okay? I don't understand…"

"After our dinner at the café." She shrugged, tying on her own apron. "He wanted to make sure we were on the same page, that this was about Nadia and he wasn't interested in anything in…*us.*"

Hands on hips, her sister scowled. "If you two aren't the most stubborn—"

But the bell over the studio door rang and the families of Crossvine Creek started arriving.

"Hey, Miss Harley." Ashley led Katie in.

"I am so glad you came." Harley set them up at the same table as Nadia. "You're a pro at this, both of you, so you might have to help Nadia and her family. Okay?"

"Helpers?" Katie asked, smiling proudly.

"Exactly." Harley patted the girl's back. "You're an excellent helper."

Before long, the room was mostly full. A lot were students and their parents, some were past students, and—surprisingly—Viola North and Bev Washington. The two women sat at the far end of the same table as Josh and his family, and Ashley and Katie.

Harley took her spot on the dais at the front of the room and smiled. "Thank you all for coming out for our family craft night. We're making a fall staple: clove apples. When you're done, you'll have something pretty to hang in your house for the rest of the year. They also make a lovely gift."

Autumn had taken a spot closest to the families with numerous small children—in case extra hands were needed.

"On your table, you should find your apples, cloves, ribbon, glue, and your skewer sticks. The skewer stick is for poking the apple only—I wanted to remind everyone of that." Harley smiled again. "Okay, Mrs. North?"

Viola North cackled. "I'm not making any promises, Harley."

The rest of the room laughed along.

"Now the key to a successful clove apple is keeping the cloves placed tightly. Like this." Harley held up her apple, used the thin bamboo skewer to poke a hole, then pressed in one of the fragrant whole cloves. She repeated the process five times. "See, they're almost on top of each other." She waited for the majority of the attendees to nod. "Let's get started, then. Once it's done, we'll attach the ribbons. So, kids, don't touch the glue."

Harley put on some calming background music and began making a slow circuit of the room. She was pleased to see Katie and Nadia working together on one apple. Katie was poking the holes and Nadia was placing the cloves—and they were both grinning from ear to ear.

Josh sat, Tucker at his side, eyeing the supplies with dubious curiosity. In that moment, his expression was so much like Nadia's, she had to smile.

"Not much into clove apples?" she asked, unable to resist.

He sighed, holding up the apple. "This is my first."

"What?" Ashley asked. "Coach, this is like—fall. It's not really fall without a couple of clove apples in the house. They make the whole house smell like—"

"Fall?" Josh asked, chuckling. "All right, here we go."

Tucker watched, shaking his head. "Here, Dad."

Harley left Josh in his son's capable hands, resisting the urge to spend extra time with Nadia and Tucker—with Josh. His eyes looked especially blue tonight. Maybe it was his chambray shirt or the stubble on his jaw or...

"Harley?" Viola North waved her over. "My fingers are a little arthritic for this. The chill makes my joints ache all the more. I think I'll just sit and take in the view, if you don't mind. I didn't want you to think I wasn't participating due to a lack of excellent instruction."

"I appreciate that, Mrs. North." She studied the older woman's hands. "Would you like some clay to work with? It's soft enough to knead, even if you don't make anything, and it might help work out some of the stiffness."

"Why, aren't you the sweetest thing?" Viola beamed up at her. "I suppose I could try."

Once Viola was situated, Harley was prepared to make another loop around the room when Bev Washington asked, "I hear Grant Maxwell is back in town and the two of you had a nice little reunion in the park?"

Harley smiled. First Autumn, now the widows. "It's nice that he's come home."

"Well, it's about time." Viola looked stern. "His daddy shouldn't work too much longer. He should be able to stay home and take care of his grandbabies."

"Grandbabies?" As far as she knew, Grant's sister was still in college—single and childless.

"Well, it's only a matter of time before we get Grant set up proper." Bev was studying her. "You two were always so sweet on each other."

"We've always been very good *friends*," Harley insisted.

"What better foundation is there for a long and happy marriage than friendship?" Bev asked. "You're too pretty not to settle down, Harley. I expect Autumn will be getting a proposal any day now. It's your turn."

Harley swallowed.

"We had thought you and Coach would make a fine couple. Both of you so good-looking, and you already being sweet on his kids. But I'm not seeing much progress there," Viola said. "It's a shame too, because those children need a mother."

Harley winced. Viola North was hard of hearing, which meant she had no idea that she was talking loud enough for everyone in the room to hear. Thankfully, it didn't look like Josh had taken any notice. "I consider Josh and his family good friends, Mrs. North." *Because he's told me that's all we can be.* "I'm sure, when the time is right, Josh will find the right woman—and so will Grant. But that woman won't be me."

Viola and Bev sighed—almost in unison.

"How's the clay?" she asked, hoping to redirect the conversation.

"Fine," Viola said, adding another sigh. "If I was thirty years younger, I'd have set my sights on Coach McBride. That's a good man, right there. A respectable job, sweet kids, nice little house—what more could a young gal want?"

Love. But Harley only shrugged in answer.

"Forty," Bev snorted. "Forty years, not thirty, Viola North. And don't you try to tell me otherwise. Besides, you'd have to fight me for him."

The two of them started laughing—the perfect time to slip away.

The class went well. Other than Katie gluing her clove apple to the table and a little boy who decided he'd rather eat his apple halfway through the craft, the afternoon went off without a hitch.

Nadia held out her clove apple. "See?"

"We did it." Katie pointed at herself, then Nadia.

"You two are quite the team." Harley nodded. "I love it."

"Mine's good." Tucker seemed pleased. "But, Dad..." He shook his head.

"What?" Josh held up his apple. "I'm not creative. Art and I don't get along."

She stepped forward, inspecting the apple. "That's not

SASHA SUMMERS

true. Everyone likes art. Some people are more intimidated by it than others. Usually people who need structure and rules." Harley took the apple. "All it needs is another row, through here."

"I told you," Tucker said. "I told him, Miss Harley." He stood. "Here."

"Thank you." She sat, wishing the chair wasn't wedged up against Josh. There was no way for her to move, not with Tucker and Katie and Nadia all squeezed in around them, watching.

"He did." Josh's words were pitched low. "Tell me, that is."

She ignored the delightful tingles caused by the deep velvet tones of his voice and bent forward to retrieve the skewer. When she sat back, she tried to perch on the edge of the chair Tucker vacated for her—as far from Josh as possible. Not that it did anything to defuse the ripple of tension in the air between them. *One he didn't feel.* She rested the fruit on the table and set about filling the empty spaces on the apple's surface with holes. "Now, all you need are the cloves." She reached for one at the same time he did. The brush of his fingers along the back of her hand triggered a full-body shudder. He didn't instantly draw back either. No, his hand rested—warm and large—on top of hers. Too long.

When his hand lifted, he picked up a clove and began pressing it into the apple.

Over and over, she reminded herself that she was only

152

seeing what she wanted to—feeling what she wanted to. *But I don't want to feel this way.* Then again, with Josh McBride, she didn't seem to have much choice.

"Looks like you've got it now." Was that her? She sounded... Well, not like herself. She glanced his way. He was staring at the apple but his jaw was clenched tight—almost angry. She cleared her throat and attempted to sound normal. "I didn't mean to hijack your project."

"He needed help." Tucker sounded so disappointed, Harley had to laugh.

Josh's brows rose, his gaze shifting her way. "You like laughing at me."

Her laugh stuck in her throat. One minute she was fine, the next she was barely breathing. And he...he was looking at her mouth. No? He wasn't looking at her at all now. Nope, he was tight-jawed all over again.

"He did need help, Miss Harley," Nadia said, climbing into her lap. "See, Daddy. She's the best helper. She makes sure everyone makes something special."

Harley hugged Nadia close. "Now you each have your first clove apple. A keepsake to remind you of tonight. Did you have fun?"

"Yes. Of course." Nadia smiled up at her. "Daddy? Did you have fun?"

"I did." Josh smiled back at his daughter. "I'll try to be more help with the baking. Number three on the list, right? Wednesday?"

"Yes." She swallowed, unable to resist his smile. It was a lovely smile. "Wednesday."

"I remember." His eyes met hers. "Your list helps."

"Miss Harley is the best." Nadia nodded, poking a clove into the apple.

Harley knew Josh was looking at her but decided now was not the best time to get lost in those blue eyes—not only because she was still recovering from the tingles but also because they had an audience. Viola North, Bev Washington, and her sister were gathered at the end of the table, watching—and up to no good.

JOSH FROWNED. BERNIE peered over the top of his legal pad, like he'd been doing for most of their Wednesday faculty meeting. He doubted Bernie had heard a thing about the mandatory lunch duties, need for club sponsorships, or new gradebook software the principal had mentioned. Clearly, his assistant coach had something else on his mind...and Josh knew he'd hear about it. But after the meeting, he had to get home to clean up, load the kids and Chewie into the Jeep, and head to the Welsh house for dinner and baking... And he was already going to be cutting things close. But he had the feeling Bernie wouldn't wait.

"What's up?" Josh asked, the minute the meeting was over.

"Now, I feel right uncomfortable about this, Josh." Bernie glanced around them. "But I felt like it was my duty to tell you this, man-to-man."

Josh was worried now. "Is everything okay, Bernie?"

"I don't know." He took a deep breath. "My wife is good friends with Jentina Ramos. She's friends with Viola North and Bev Washington. And well, there's talk about your Miss Welsh being paired up with someone else."

That was the very last thing he'd expected to hear from his no-nonsense assistant coach.

"I know how sweet on her you are. I know what I walked in on, too. Sorry about that." He shook his head. "Real sorry about that. Plus, she is good with those kids. I think you two would make a fine couple—a fine family. But those widows..." He broke off, shaking his head. "When they make up their minds, it's a done deal. They get it done."

"Bernie, I appreciate it—"

"Of course." Bernie went on, "I just don't want Miss Welsh stolen away from you. Wouldn't be right. I don't care what they say, you and she are a better fit than her and that Grant Maxwell fellow. It was years back, but he played football. One of those kids who thinks they know just about everything, all the time." He shook his head. "No, sir. I told my wife, too, how you two didn't need anyone nudging or poking at you. These things should happen on their own."

Josh didn't argue. He was a private man. The idea of Viola North, Bev Washington, or anyone attempting to steer the course of his love life didn't sit well with him.

"Still. Time isn't slowing down. Don't sit back too long, Josh, or you might just lose her. And that would be a shame." He clapped Josh on the shoulder. "You think on it. I guess I'll see you in the morning."

Josh wasn't sure what to do with his assistant coach's advice. Or Viola North's not so quiet statement that his kids needed a mother. He barely knew these people and, somehow, they all felt qualified to air their opinion about his family.

He was tired and frustrated and seriously rethinking spending the evening baking with Harley Welsh—rethinking the whole checklist, really. Again. The two of them spending time together would only add to the talk, not to mention how his brain tended to short-circuit when Harley was around. He'd been making arts and crafts, surrounded by his kids, and he'd still contemplated kissing her. All from one touch. Just the feel of her soft skin beneath his fingertips and he was done for.

Bernie had meant well but the truth of the matter was Josh couldn't *lose her to Grant Maxwell.* He didn't have Harley. At all.

He opened the front door to find the kids sitting on the floor, waiting. Chewie lay on the floor between them.

"Ready?" Nadia hopped up.

No.

"I finished my homework," Tucker said. "That way, we

don't have to rush tonight."

Great.

"Hi, Coach." Mrs. Reed, coat on and purse in hand, was headed for the door. "I hear you're making apple dumplings tonight. I told Nadia there is nothing better than vanilla ice cream with a fresh-from-the-oven dumpling."

"She bought us some to take tonight." Nadia smiled, holding up the insulated shopping bag.

"That's very thoughtful of you, Mrs. Reed." What would he do without her?

"Nadia promised me an apple dumpling. It's Mr. Reed's favorite." Mrs. Reed gave Nadia a quick hug. "You have fun." She waved on her way out.

"Come on, Dad." Tucker stood. "You don't want to be late."

"Don't I even have time for a shower?" he asked, glancing at the clock on the wall. They were already late. "Guess not." They loaded up and made the short drive to the Welshes' house. Even before he'd seen the street number, he'd known the place where Harley lived. The mint-green with bright white trim cottage was nestled in what promised to be an impressive garden in the spring and summer. But it was the colorfully painted clay creatures throughout the yard, the decorated porch and railing, as well as the painted stepping stones that gave it away.

"Miss Harley lives here?" Nadia asked, staring up at the house. "It's so pretty."

Chewie rested his paws on the white picket fence, sniffing the air.

"He smells Cobie," Tucker said.

Cobie, Baxter, and Chewie had made fast friends at the dog park. After the initial sniff-down, the three of them had happily chased balls, played tug-of-war, and rolled in the dirt until it was time to part ways.

Now, Cobie and Baxter came tearing out the front door and down the stairs, barking—with tails wagging.

"Come on in. Everyone is here to help out." Harley stood on the porch, waving them inside. "Dinner is ready." She wore an apron over her jeans and mustard-colored sweater. Her hair was in a loose bun at the base of her neck, long tendrils curling around her face. The face. The smile. "Hope you're hungry."

She looked beautiful. As always.

Chewie, Baxter, and Cobie gave each other a quick hello before tearing after each other—up the front steps.

"Dogs coming through," Harley called out.

"Hear that?" Tucker gave him a disapproving look. "Dinner's ready cuz we're late."

"Are you?" Harley asked. "I didn't notice. Come inside."

Everyone meant Harley's whole family. But, as Harley had pointed out, the list was a family tradition so that made sense. Josh had begun to expect a sort of orderly chaos when the Welshes were together. Like now. Everyone was moving—everyone had a job. Autumn and Noah were setting a large table on the back porch. Cynthia was pouring wine while James Welsh carried a basket of rolls in one hand and a salad bowl in the other.

"We brought ice cream." Nadia held out the bag. "Mrs. Reed says you have to have it with apple dumplings."

"Mrs. Reed is correct." Harley took the bag, pulled out the ice cream, and put it in the freezer. "For later."

"We're supposed to bring her one," Tucker said. "It's Mr. Reed's favorite."

"Well, then we'll have to make a double batch so there's one left." Harley's brown eyes were fixed on the kids. Not him. "I hope you're all ready to bake?"

"What can I do?" Josh asked.

"Grab those pot holders, will you?" Autumn asked. "Noah put the trivets on the table already. We just need to carry the lasagna out of the oven."

Josh opened the oven, and the odor of garlic and oregano and Parmesan wafted out into the room. "Smells good."

"It is good. Harley makes the best lasagna ever," Autumn assured him. "She uses extra cheese."

"I like cheese," Nadia said.

"And her homemade garlic knots," Cynthia added. "They are so good. All those carbs are dangerous for the hips and thighs though."

"I don't know what you're talking about." Autumn shook her head.

"Me neither." James Welsh caught Cynthia's hand in his.

Josh carried the large pan of lasagna onto the back porch and placed it on the waiting trivets. He stepped back, taking in the deep wide-planked wraparound porch that overlooked a large green yard. More shrubs and flower beds lined the wooden privacy fence—along with several more ceramic creations. "This is really nice."

"It is," Noah agreed.

"What's that?" Josh asked, pointing to the building at the back of the lot. It looked like a replica of the main house—with extra windows and a roll-top garage door.

"That is Noah's latest renovation." Autumn leaned against Noah. "Our home studio. With perfect lighting and just the right amount of space and—"

"What she's trying to say is, it's perfect." Harley was smiling.

"Well it is." Autumn sat beside Noah.

Everyone sat, plates were passed, and conversation paused long enough for everyone to enjoy the first few bites of dinner.

"This is yummy." Nadia speared another bite of pasta onto her fork.

"Just be thankful Harley cooked and not me," Autumn said, laughing. "I'm not nearly as talented in the kitchen."

Josh saw the sisters look at each other and burst out laughing—their father too. Sitting there, watching the Welsh family, he felt included. His kids had no problem diving into conversation, too. James asked Tucker all about his classes, who his teachers were, and what he thought of Crossvine Creek. Once Tucker got warmed up, he chattered away for the remainder of dinner. Even Nadia was coaxed into the discussion, and she joined in, talking about her artwork, junior cheer club, and Katie. A lot about Katie—which set Josh's heart at ease. She'd had energy to spare at the clove apple class—but Nadia had soaked it up like a sponge. What more could a father want? His kids happy? With friends? Being kids? Things were falling into place—faster than he'd anticipated.

Thanks to Harley.

He knew better, but he still glanced her way. She was listening intently to Tucker, leaning toward him and nodding at whatever he was saying. Did she know how his kids came to life when she was around? Could she understand the impact she'd made on all of them? Whether or not she was interested in him, he knew—without a doubt—that she cared about his kids.

Nadia finished another garlic knot and shifted in her seat, peering over Noah's shoulder at the dogs playing in the grass nearby. "Chewie is having fun, too," she said, placing her little hand on his arm. "See, Daddy?"

"I see." He pressed a quick kiss to her temple. "Looks like you are, as well. You like lasagna?"

She nodded, holding up a bite. "It's yummy. Miss Harley, can you teach Daddy how to make this? Please?"

Harley wrinkled her nose. "I don't know, Nadia. It's a

161

top-secret recipe."

"Oh." Nadia looked very serious all of a sudden. "Hm…Daddy, can you keep a secret?"

Josh chuckled. "I don't know. There's a high demand for top-secret lasagna recipes. I might try to sell it and retire early."

"Daddy," Nadia sighed. "Never mind, Miss Harley. Don't tell him."

The whole table laughed.

Dinnertime talk covered a wide range of topics. Josh learned that Noah's next renovation and restoration project was the county courthouse—right here in Crossvine Creek. Harley and Autumn discussed a few craft ideas for the holiday season, and James and Cynthia were planning to host their first joint Thanksgiving.

"What are your Thanksgiving plans?" Cynthia asked.

"I haven't thought that far ahead. We'll be making some new traditions this year." Josh winked at Tucker, then Nadia. "Maybe we'll just have ice cream all day."

"Really?" Nadia was wide-eyed with excitement. "*All* day?"

"No. He's teasing, Squirt." Tucker shook his head, then paused to look his way. "You're teasing, right?"

"I am." Josh added, "But—after turkey—I think we can add ice cream to the menu."

Tucker nodded.

"You are more than welcome to join us, Coach." Cynthia

passed the basket of garlic knots back around the table. "I'm sure we'll have plenty of food and Chewie would be welcome too—he's made such fast friends with Baxter and Cobie, after all."

Josh sat back in his chair, genuinely surprised by the invitation. "That's very kind of you, Cynthia, but—"

"No buts." She waved her hand, dismissing his arguments. "Just think on it." Then she lowered her voice, but whispered loudly enough for everyone to hear her add, "Kids, I'll make sure we have extra ice cream."

Nadia giggled. "Thank you, Miss Cynthia."

Josh smiled at his daughter.

The cleanup was a joint effort—an additional flurry of chaotic activity that wound up being surprisingly effective. James made coffee, Autumn helped Tucker and Nadia make their own glasses of chocolate milk, and Harley had him carry the dessert plates out onto the porch—carrying a large apple pie and the ice cream Nadia had brought with them.

"I'm not sure I'll be able to move after this." Josh sipped his coffee. "Let alone make apple dumplings."

"That's fine." Harley had done an excellent job of minimizing eye contact tonight, he'd noticed. "After the lasagna recipe comment, I'm not sure you should. Tucker, Nadia, Autumn, and I can do it."

"Um…" Autumn cast her sister a doubtful look.

"Fine, Nadia, Tucker, *Noah* and I can do it." Harley nodded.

"I mean, I'll help cut apples and measure things but you know pastry and I don't have the best relationship." Autumn sipped her coffee. "Unless it's eating pastry. No problems there."

There was no missing the adoration between Noah and Autumn. For that matter, Cynthia and James were pretty smitten with one another. He'd lost Bethany so long ago, it was hard to remember what that was like... Having that connection with someone—that unspoken understanding that filled silence with peace and warmth. Even with his mother there, helping day in and day out, it wasn't the same. And even though he'd done a good job of pretending the hole in his heart and in his life didn't exist, sometimes it was harder than others.

Like now.

Looking at Harley wasn't a conscious choice. It just...happened. She was smiling—watching her sister and father, happy for them. But for one unguarded moment, there was longing on her face. Her gaze fell to her empty dessert plate, her lashes fluttering against her cheeks—and then her topaz eyes locked with his.

Something told him that if she ever changed her mind about them, she'd more than fill the hole in his life—and in his heart, too.

Chapter Nine

HARLEY STEPPED ONE foot inside the Corner Brew and Bakery and heard her name.

"Harley." Grant Maxwell sat at one of the small tables, a cup of coffee, a half-eaten muffin, and a newspaper spread out before him.

"Good morning." She accepted his hug. "It's so great that you're back, Grant." He was one of those friends she'd always been able to rely on. They could go months without speaking and still pick up right where they'd left off the last time they were together.

"Join me?" he asked, draping his arm across her shoulder. "It's on me. Anything you want."

"Big spender, huh?" She laughed. "I'll stay—but I'll pay for my own breakfast."

He shook his head. "Always so obstinate."

"Me?" She pushed against his chest. "Do you *know* you?"

Grant laughed, hugging her close.

"Excuse me," someone said, behind them. She knew that voice. Low and gruff and instantly setting her nerves on high alert.

Harley pulled away from Grant and spun to face Josh. "Hi."

He barely spared her a glance. There was no hint of a smile on his handsome, stiff face.

"Are we blocking the way?" Grant frowned. "Sorry, man. Sorry. Happy to see my girl—you know how it is."

Josh nodded, but he still didn't smile. Or look at her.

"Have you two met?" Harley asked, an unexpected tightness in her stomach. Last night had ended on a high note. At least, she'd thought so. They'd made two dozen apple dumplings, laughed the whole time, and she'd been very proud of her self-control. Barely any ogling—at least, not that Josh had seen. So why was he acting so...so wound up now?

"No?" Grant smiled but there was a slight furrow on his brow. Then again, it was hard to miss the hostility rolling off of Josh.

"Let me introduce you. Josh McBride, our new high school coach. Grant Maxwell, lawyer." Harley waited, watching the two men shake hands.

"You're the man responsible for turning this place into a football town, I hear?" Grant asked.

"I don't know about that," Josh said.

"Don't let him fool you, Grant. Coach, here, is the best thing that's ever happened to the Crossvine Creek Wild Cats," Arnie called from behind the counter. "Our boys have never looked so good or played so hard."

"High praise," Grant said. "Arnie eats, sleeps, and breathes football."

Josh's smile was reluctant, but it eased the tension. "I appreciate that, Arnie."

"We've got the donuts ready to go, Coach." Arnie grinned. "On Miss Harley, of course."

"When did you become a football fan?" Grant looked at her like she'd sprung a second head.

More of a Josh McBride fan. "Since now." She shrugged.

Josh was doing that expressionless staring thing again. It had been a while since he'd done that. She'd thought, hoped, that they'd established a friendship. "The boys appreciate it. Bernie too."

She smiled, the steadiness of his gaze adding twenty pounds of pressure to her chest. "Good. I'm glad." She swallowed.

"Enjoy your breakfast." Josh nodded. "Good to meet you." He tilted his head Grant's way, collected the boxes of donuts, and left.

"He's...intense." Grant frowned, leading Harley toward the bakery counter. "Is he always so *hospitable?*"

"Coach is a good man." Arnie leaned against the countertop. "Not much of a talker, but that's all right. These days, people talk too much. He cares about those kids and he gets the job done. I've got no complaints."

"Makes sense." Grant nodded. "What are you having?"

Breakfast was a bit of a blur. Harley picked at her pumpkin cream cheese muffin and let her coffee go cold all while Grant filled her in on his move and his ideas for his father's law firm. As nice as it was to visit with him, she couldn't shake the feeling that Josh was *angry*. With her?

"Why do I get the feeling you haven't heard a thing I've said?" Grant asked, leaning back in the café chair, his brow creasing in question.

"I did," she lied, shoving a piece of muffin into her mouth.

"Uh-huh." Grant leaned forward, propping his elbows on the table to stare at her. "You'll tell me. You always tell me."

She ate some more muffin. There was nothing to tell. She had feelings for the grumpy new coach, only he did not return them. Not exactly exciting breakfast conversation.

"You're going to choke." He laughed—but he didn't move. "Spill."

The cold coffee made her wince, which earned her more laughter from Grant. "I don't know what you're talking about."

"Okay. Fine." He shrugged. "I guess I'm just losing my touch."

"I'm sorry, Grant." She was, too. She spent too much time worrying over Josh McBride and his mood swings. "I promise next time, you will have my undivided attention. Okay?"

"I'll hold you to that." He paused. "Everything is okay?"

"Oh, yes, sure. It's all great." *My heart hurts.* The thing was, she didn't even know when her heart had gotten involved…

"Yeah, that was convincing." The furrow on his brow deepened. "*Not.*"

She smiled. "You and your sarcasm."

"You missed it?" he asked. "You don't have to say it, I know you did."

She laughed.

"So, now that you're a big football fan, are you free Friday night for the homecoming game?" He shrugged. "Dad was talking to me about providing some sponsorship to the team so I figured I'd go to a game."

"I'll be there." She'd promised Nadia and confirmed with Josh mid-apple dumpling baking. "You're more than welcome to sit with us."

His eyebrows rose so high, they almost disappeared into his hairline. "You'll be there? Who are you and what have you done with Harley Welsh?"

"Oh hush." She swallowed. "I've been helping Coach McBride with his little girl, Nadia. The move here kind of threw her for a loop and she's having a hard time connecting. She's precious, Grant, just precious—you'll see. And she's an *amazing* little sculptor, too. Far beyond her age." She avoided his gaze. "Autumn and I have been going to the games, cheering with her, generally—"

"You've always had a big heart, Harley." He smiled. "Always."

"Yeah, well, it's a problem." She rolled her eyes.

"No, Oliver was the problem. Oliver was a d—"

"Let's not talk about any of that, okay?" She hurried to cut him off.

"Okay. If you're spending time with this little girl, I guess that means you're still not dating?"

She glared at him. "Subtle."

"I wasn't trying to be. You need to move on." He sighed. "Now I'm going to ask you something and I'm counting on you to keep it between you and me. I don't need the whole town to know."

"You have my full attention." She waited, watching a slow wash of red color his cheeks.

"Is Dalia Ramirez single?" he asked, smiling. "I ran into her at the Farmer's Market."

"Oh, you did?" Harley leaned forward, grinning. "She is. And she's as sweet as ever." Which was true. The town librarian was about to get swept off her feet—Grant never did anything 'small.' Harley could hardly wait to see how things played out between the two of them. "That was fast work. You didn't even give the widows a chance to offer up a list of candidates."

"I'll pass, thanks." He shrugged. "I don't know. There was that...spark?" He let his shoulders fall. "If that makes sense?"

"It does." She nodded. *I know all about the spark.* "Well,

if you decide not to take Dalia to the game, you're welcome to join us. And if you do decide to ask Dalia to the game, you can both join us."

"Not sure that's the vibe I want for a first date."

"What? My loud family? A high school football game? The entire town whispering about you?" She laughed. "But then again, you might remember how loud I get at football games—"

"Still?" Grant looked horrified. "I thought you did that as a joke?"

"Now I do it to have fun." She crossed her arms over her chest. "So, you know, if that impacts your decision to try to romance someone while I'm screaming—it's something to consider." She glanced at the clock. "I'm out of time. Class starts in…ten minutes." It was Thursday so Nadia would be there.

"I'll walk you there."

It was a short walk to Welsh Studios, but Grant had her laughing the whole time. When they arrived, Grant came in, said good morning to Autumn, and admired the changes they'd made since the last time he'd visited. As soon as the school bus stopped out front, he slipped out.

"What was that?" Autumn whispered, holding open one of the doors for the students.

"Grant? An accidental breakfast." She held open the other door. Telling her sister about Grant's interest in Dalia was a bad idea. As much as she adored her sister, Harley was fairly certain Autumn wouldn't be able to keep that sort of information to herself. If she shared it with Cynthia...well, then the widows would find out, then all of Crossvine Creek.

Class was a great diversion. Harley suspected her sister was pondering all sorts of meanings behind her accidental breakfast with Grant—that was just the way Autumn worked.

"Miss Harley." Nadia waved her over. "Junior cheer club is next week."

Katie's fingertips were dripping glue.

"Oh, Katie, here." Harley handed her a wet wipe. "Remember, use the cotton swab. Not your fingers. Or you might stick to the table."

Katie giggled, wiping her fingertips off.

"Are you excited about cheer club?" Harley asked.

"And my uniform." Nadia nodded. "But can I use your pom-poms this week?"

"Of course," Harley agreed.

"And will you come with me to cheer club next week?" Nadia asked, her blue eyes so like her father's.

No more thinking about Josh. Or worrying about why he was upset this morning. Or hoping he was okay. She sighed inwardly.

Nadia continued, "You help me yell better."

Katie grinned. "You yell real loud, Miss Harley."

"Thank you." Harley laughed. "I'll talk to your father about cheer club, okay?" After this weekend, her time with

Nadia would consist of class and Friday night football games. With luck, they'd make it into the state finals and there'd be plenty of more games in their future. If not…well, she didn't want to think about that. Time with Nadia had become important to her. She loved the little girl—Tucker, too.

"Okay. I will too." Nadia went back to carefully applying glue to her small pumpkin. Once it was ready, they'd sprinkle glitter all over it. This was Autumn's idea—Harley wasn't a huge fan of glitter. It was a pain to clean up. "I'm making this for Chewie."

"I think Chewie will love it. Just make sure he doesn't eat it." Harley was pretty sure a pumpkin covered in glue and glitter wasn't a healthy snack option for a dog.

"It might make him sick." Nadia frowned. "I'll put it where he can see it, but not eat it."

"Good idea," Harley agreed, moving on to a little boy who'd managed to glue his shirt to his pumpkin.

After class was over, Autumn asked, "Who's idea was this?" She was scraping globs of glue and glitter from the laminate tabletops.

"Yours." Harley pointed at her. "All yours. You know how I feel about glitter."

"It's magical?" Autumn asked, laughing.

"If by magical, you mean it's horrible, then yes." Harley continued scraping at the next long table. "I'm not sure where most of the glitter wound up—on the pumpkins or the students. Luckily, I got to Katie before she dumped the glitter in her hair." Harley shook her head. "You know who she reminds me of?"

Autumn shook her head.

"You. One hundred percent you," Harley said as she sprayed disinfectant on the tables.

Autumn shrugged. "That's why she and Nadia have become best friends. Because little Nadia is you. And boy, does that little girl adore you."

Harley smiled. She was okay with that. "The feeling is mutual."

"I wish Josh McBride was handsome *and* smart," Autumn sighed.

"What does that mean?" Harley waited, spray in hand.

"If he was smart, he'd adore you, too. I mean, I don't care what he said, it's *obvious* he *really* likes you." Autumn held up her hand. "No, seriously. Noah and I kept track. Every time you weren't looking at him, he was looking at you."

"You kept track?" She blinked.

"It was Noah's idea." Autumn smiled. "He's a numbers kind of guy."

"Unbelievable." Harley went back to cleaning off the table tops. "I hate to burst your bubble but I ran into him this morning and he was not happy to see me. At all. He looked ready to bite my head off, in fact. He even intimidated Grant—and you know how hard that is to do."

"He ran into you and Grant at your accidental breakfast?" Autumn was entirely focused on her glue scraping. "And he was upset?" She glanced at Harley. "Interesting. I wonder why."

Harley shrugged. She'd pretty much spent the entire morning wondering the same thing.

"I DON'T KNOW what's eating you, but I hope things get straightened out," Bernie said, giving him a parting wave on his way out for the evening.

Josh leaned back in his chair, ran a hand along the back of his neck, and took a deep breath. The team had worked harder than ever. If he said jump, they jumped. If he ran drills, they did it until he was happy with their time. Did he praise them? Give them encouragement? Not today. He'd barked and scowled and been the worst kind of coach. And it had nothing to do with them.

Seeing Harley Welsh wrapped up and laughing in Grant Maxwell's arms had gutted him—plain and simple. If Arnie hadn't seen him, he'd have turned around and left. Instead, he'd shaken hands with the man who'd removed any chance of Harley ever developing feelings for him. Grant and Harley had a history. Grant made her laugh and smile—she hadn't even noticed he'd been standing there. All he and Harley shared was a love of Nadia.

He'd stomped in here, slammed things around, growled

orders and generally been unbearable to a group of kids who gave their all for him.

He slumped forward, resting his elbows on his desk. Taking out his heartache on his students wasn't okay—he shouldn't take it out on anyone. What happened today, his attitude on the field and in class, wasn't going to happen again. *Not getting what you want is part of life.* It was a lesson he knew all too well.

Seeing Harley with Grant would get easier, in time. At least she was happy. That was something. He needed to remember that he'd been the one to tell her there was no romantic future for them—before she'd assured him she wasn't interested. He sighed and pushed out of his seat.

His phone buzzed with a message from Mrs. Reed. She'd forgotten yogurt and pretzels for the kids' lunches and needed him to stop by the grocery store on the way home. He texted back, packed his things into his duffel bag, and headed to his Jeep. The drive to the local grocer's was quick—a drive anywhere in Crossvine Creek was quick. He parked and headed inside, a man on a mission.

One thing small-town living was teaching him was patience. As a coach, he was used to getting extra attention now and then. But here, he couldn't set foot in any restaurant, store, or even walk Chewie through Town Square Park without a handful of football enthusiasts rushing up with questions or praise or offering to bring his family food. He had more casseroles in the freezer than he knew what to do with.

Josh had just disentangled himself from old man Krieger, who had a lot to say about the team they were playing Friday night, when he felt a hand on his shoulder.

"Hey." It was Noah. "How long does it normally take you to buy a loaf of bread?" He glanced after Mr. Krieger's retreating form.

"A while." Josh chuckled. "I'm looking for yogurt and pretzels and I haven't even made it past the produce section."

"I'll use my cart to block you." Noah turned his cart and led the way.

"So, this Pumpkin Patch Fall Festival this weekend…" Josh said. "It's a big deal?"

"Yup." Noah nodded. "Small towns take their festivals seriously."

"I'm getting that." Josh had been informed at the last faculty meeting that the coach always took a turn in the dunking booth. Since he knew how important tradition was, he didn't argue. After today, his whole team would probably line up for a chance to knock him into the water.

"I was never really into this sort of thing but Autumn has this way of making things…fun," Noah said. "I bet your kids are excited."

"That's all they've talked about pretty much all week." He stared at the wall of pretzels. "Why are there so many kinds of pretzels?"

Noah ran a hand over his head, equally surprised. "I have

no idea."

Josh grabbed a bag and held it out. Noah shrugged. He tucked the bag under his arm. "Next." They moved on, a question hovering on the edges of his mind. One that wouldn't let go. One he shouldn't ask. "Do you know Grant Maxwell?" *What am I doing?*

"Some. I was a few years older, but he, Harley and Autumn were pretty close." Noah looked his way. "Autumn said he's back now. A lawyer, like his father."

"I guess so. Harley was having breakfast with him this morning." Which made it clear why he was asking about Grant Maxwell. He scrambled for something more, something that wouldn't automatically make it clear he was asking about Harley and Grant—even if that was exactly what he was doing. "Mr. Maxwell, senior, called about sponsoring new helmets for the team."

"That's good. The team deserves it." Noah turned his cart at the dairy case, walked down the open coolers, and stopped. "Yogurt?"

"Yogurt." And here he'd thought the pretzel assortment was overwhelming. He had no idea what he was looking for. "This is ridiculous."

"Can I ask you something?" Noah asked.

"Sure." He pulled out his phone to text Mrs. Reed for yogurt clarification.

"You and Harley?"

Josh almost dropped his phone.

Noah noticed. He gave Josh a look full of sympathy. And understanding.

Guess I haven't done such a good job of hiding my feelings after all. He braced himself.

"You two seem to be...wary of each other." Noah crossed his arms over his chest. "I'm guessing you've heard something about New York?"

"Not much." Josh cleared his throat. "What I've pieced together is some guy treated her badly and ended it because she didn't want kids?"

"The first part is right." Noah frowned. "But Harley wants kids."

Josh froze, his heart slamming into his rib cage so hard his chest hurt. "She does?"

"She loves kids." Noah leveled him with a hard look. "She loves your kids. Is that what the holdup is?"

Josh stared right back, oddly defensive. "No. She told me she's not interested."

"What?" Noah's frown grew. "Harley? She said that?"

Josh went back to looking at yogurt, his heart hammering in his chest. *She'd said it.* He grabbed a box of yogurt pouches that looked vaguely familiar—eager to head home.

"Who told you she didn't want kids?" Noah looked perplexed.

He tried to replay their conversation. She had, hadn't she? But then, she'd been a little surprised when her hug of comfort had led to his sudden let's-stay-friends declaration

179

outside of the Main Street Café. "I guess I misunderstood."

Noah sighed. "Maybe you two should consider having that conversation again. All of it."

Josh shoved his phone into his pocket, refusing to consider even the slightest chance that Noah was right, that he'd misunderstood Harley. He didn't want to hurt her. He didn't want to hurt the kids. But he didn't want to get hurt, either.

"I'm leaving this stuff to Autumn from now on." Noah nodded. "That was awkward. It'll never happen again."

"Okay." Josh chuckled.

"So, poker night." Noah launched into who played, where they played, and how they all hoped he'd join them next Tuesday night.

Josh did his best to engage but the seeds of doubt had been planted. All the things he'd managed to suppress were pushing back. Things like hope and want and…love. He couldn't let one ten-second conversation change the facts. Loving Harley Welsh was a risk—for all of them.

By the time he got home, he was worn out. Apparently, it showed.

"What's the matter, Daddy?" Nadia asked, holding up her arms.

He picked her up. "I had a long day. But it's better now." He hugged her close, tickling her sides until she was giggling.

"Let me take that." Mrs. Reed took the brown paper grocery sack. "Dinner will be ready in five minutes."

"Thank you, Mrs. Reed." He smiled at the older woman. "I don't say that often enough."

"Well, now, there's no need. You've the sweetest children I've ever met and we get on so well." She put the groceries away and went back to cooking.

Nadia twined her little arms around his neck. "You needed a hug?"

"Always." He hugged her back. "You have a good day?"

"Yes. I saw Miss Harley." She was all smiles. "We painted a pumpkin with glue and sprinkled it with glitter. I made it for Chewie. But he can only look at it—not eat it. I don't want him to get sick." She waited for his nod. "Miss Harley had to stop Katie from putting glitter in her hair, like a fairy. And then Matthew, he's in my class, glued his shirt to his pumpkin."

He let Nadia chatter away. For the first time, she had stories about her class, lunch in the cafeteria, and playing chase with Katie and some other girls at recess. Art class still topped the list, but it wasn't the only thing she was talking about. "Sounds like you had a good day."

She nodded. "And Mrs. Reed made some chicken fingers for dinner, too."

"And you love chicken fingers." He glanced over Tucker's shoulder at the worksheets on the table. "History?"

"Geography. Making a map," Tucker said. "I'm going to make it really detailed." He tapped the end of his pencil against the textbook. "Might be up late."

Josh ruffled his hair. "Let's see how much you get done." While Tucker excelled at math and science, he loved history and geography most. But Tucker was also a perfectionist, which meant he'd stay up all night making sure every river and boundary and mountain range was just right.

"Miss Harley brought back our shopping bag," Nadia said, pointing. "She said we forgot it at her house."

Harley had stopped by?

"She also brought some divine-smelling cinnamon rolls," Mrs. Reed added. "That girl is so thoughtful. Always has been. I taught her, you know? Back in high school. She was on the shy side, but was always so thoughtful and kind."

"She is," Nadia agreed. "And pretty."

"That she is," Mrs. Reed said.

She's beautiful. He drew in a deep breath, easing the pressure in his chest. Josh had a hard time imagining Harley as shy. She seemed so...confident. "Was Autumn a year older than her?"

Mrs. Reed nodded. "They were always together. That Grant Maxwell, too."

Josh stifled a sigh, pressed a kiss to Nadia's soft cheek, and set her on the couch next to Chewie. He gave the dog a scratch behind the ear. "I met him today."

"I heard he was back. Goodness, he was a handful. Still is, I imagine. And quite the heartbreaker, too." Mrs. Reed laughed. "I wonder how long it will take before Viola North has him married off and settled. That woman is a force of nature." She winked at him. "I'm surprised she hasn't tried to pair you off with someone."

"What's that mean? To play games?" Nadia asked.

"It means a girlfriend," Tucker explained.

"Oh." Nadia stared up at him.

This was not a conversation he wanted to have in front of his kids and Mrs. Reed. This was not a conversation he wanted to have, period. "She probably realizes she'd be wasting her time." Josh shook his head. "Dinner smells good, Mrs. Reed."

"Viola North. Is that the old lady who was using clay at Miss Harley's place?" Tucker asked, looking up from his worksheets. "She was whispering with our neighbor."

Mrs. Reed perked up at that.

Josh sighed. "If she was whispering—"

"Not for you to hear," Nadia finished.

"Exactly," Josh agreed.

Mrs. Reed deflated.

"She was talking about you." Tucker shrugged. "You're *my* dad. I listened."

"That makes perfect sense, Tucker," Mrs. Reed said. "Looking out for your father, like a good boy."

"I thought so." Tucker smiled at Mrs. Reed, then looked his way—tapping his pencil again. "I did hear a few things."

"Let's wash up for dinner." Josh shook his head. "You've got that map to finish and I promised Nadia she could read her story to me." He turned to Mrs. Reed—her disappointment almost comical. "Thanks again for dinner."

"Of course, Coach," Mrs. Reed said. "I'm sure I'll run into you at the Pumpkin Patch Fall Festival this weekend, right?"

Nadia clapped her hands. "I'm so excited."

"I hear Coach will be in the dunking booth," Mrs. Reed said, collecting her things and storing them in her large purse.

"And the pie-eating contest." Tucker laughed. "This will be fun."

"Gosh, thanks." But Josh was laughing too.

Mrs. Reed said her good nights, the three of them sat down to dinner, and Tucker filled them in on the details of his day. Tucker had picked up another of the chicken fingers when he asked, "Dad, why can't Miss Harley be your girlfriend?"

Nadia's eyes grew wide. "Yes, Daddy. We love Miss Harley. Make her your girlfriend."

"He can't make her, Nadia," Tucker said. "She has to want to be his girlfriend."

"Oh." Nadia frowned. "Can you make her want to be your girlfriend, Daddy? Please?"

Josh swallowed the chicken that was firmly lodged in his throat. "Well..." This was officially uncharted territory.

"You could *try* to, I don't know—try to get her to like you? She likes me and Nadia, already. And Chewie. That might help you." Tucker sighed. "I mean, she *is* pretty. And nice. And creative. And pretty. And she's a really good cook." Tucker was ticking each item off on his fingers.

"You said pretty twice," Josh teased—even though he agreed with his son.

"Well, she is *pretty* pretty." Nadia was staring up at him with wide eyes. "And she makes me happy, Daddy," Nadia finished. "We love her. Lots. Right?"

Tucker nodded.

Josh sat back in his chair and blew out a long, slow breath. He didn't need his children to tell him all the wonderful things that made Harley special. He knew. His heart knew. And while hearing his children were in favor of Harley being his girlfriend did remove a few obstacles, it also added pressure. No matter what Noah had implied, it didn't make sense for him to get his hopes up. Now this. His kids campaigning for Harley to be his girlfriend? Now he wasn't the only one at risk for real hurt. "You know I care a great deal about Harley. But I think the two of us are supposed to stay friends."

"Miss North said she'd marry Grant somebody. But if she does, she won't spend time with us like she does now." Tucker was frowning.

"But she's *my* Miss Harley. I want Miss Harley to go to cheer camp and do art and braid my hair, Daddy." Nadia poked at her chicken tenders. "Don't you love her, too?"

He swallowed hard. *Yes, I love her.* "You two are worrying about something that's not happening. Miss Harley isn't getting married. She's cheering with you at the homecoming game tomorrow night and going to the festival with us this weekend. You don't need to worry. Okay?"

But he'd been warned about Viola North's matchmaking powers too many times not to worry. He had two choices. He could take Noah's advice and risk another heart-crushing conversation with Harley or he could stand by and hope she and Grant Maxwell would be very happy together. Deep down, he knew what he had to do.

Big risks lead to big rewards. Or heartbreak. Either way, he was going big.

Chapter Ten

HARLEY WALKED ACROSS the parking lot, holding the small Wild Cat homecoming mum she'd made for Nadia in one hand and a purple-and-gold thick fleece throw in the other. She'd found just the right size white silk flower, yards of colored ribbon, and small plastic trinkets to tie to it to create the mum. As far as Texas homecoming mums went, it was modest...but just right for Nadia. She hoped Nadia would like it.

But Harley's excitement wasn't just about the homecoming mum for Nadia or getting to see Josh or the game itself—though the overall buzz of the crowded stands was contagious. Harley had a secret. A life-changing, amazing, heart-filling secret. She glanced down at her watch. Any minute now, Noah was going to drop down on one knee and propose to her big sister. Noah had whisked Autumn away on a surprise date. Well, it had been a surprise to Autumn but Noah had given her a heads-up and asked for her help to pull off a romantic picnic in Town Square Park. Poor Noah was so nervous but Harley had no doubt about what her sister's answer would be.

"Miss Harley!" Nadia's call reached her over the noise of the crowd. "Miss Harley."

Harley smiled and waved, hurrying toward the sideline where Nadia waited. "Hey, Nadia." She returned the little girl's hug. "How are you? Ready to cheer?"

Nadia smiled up at her. "Yes."

"Where is Tucker?"

"He's with his friends," Nadia said.

"That's okay. Maybe we can see if Katie can sit with us?" Harley crouched. "But wait, you're missing something."

"I am?" Nadia stared down at her bright purple sweatshirt, polka-dot-covered pants, and lace-up boots. "What?"

"This." Harley held up the mum. "Every cheerleader needs a mum."

Nadia's eyes were perfect blue circles, fixed on the mum as if it was a precious treasure. "Miss Harley..." There was awe in her voice. "It's beautiful."

"I'm glad you like it." She moved the ribbons aside, showing off each of the plastic gold bits and bobs tied to the ends. She'd had fun hunting down just the right pieces to make Nadia's mum extra special. "This is a paintbrush because you like to paint. Here's a dog, for Chewie. And a football, for your dad. And a little bird for Lolly. And a bear wearing a shirt that says brother—"

"Tucker." She smiled. "And a cheerleader and Wild Cat paw prints," she added, holding out the white ribbon speckled with tiny gold paw prints. "And an 'N' for me." She pointed at the extra sparkly letter 'N' Harley had affixed to the white silk carnation all the ribbons were attached to.

"Want to wear it?" Harley asked, waiting for Nadia's whispered 'yes' before pinning the mum to the little girl's sweatshirt. "Is it too heavy?"

Nadia shook her head, still utterly transfixed by her mum. "It's perfect, Miss Harley." She threw her arms around Harley's neck and held on tight.

"You're welcome, sweetie." Harley hugged her back. She loved this little girl, so much. And right now, her heart was so full.

"You two look like you're up to something." Josh's voice pulled them apart, his gaze bouncing between the two of them. "Everything okay?"

"Look, Daddy," Nadia gushed, spinning to show him. "Miss Harley made it for me. For *me*. Isn't it beautiful?"

Harley couldn't stop smiling. "I don't think I've ever had such a positive review for something I've made."

Josh knelt, thoroughly inspecting the mum. "You made this?"

"Miss Harley can make anything. See, this?" Nadia moved another ribbon. "And Tucker? And Lolly, too. This one is for you, Daddy."

"It is homecoming. Every cheerleader needs a mum." Harley stood, beyond thrilled that Nadia loved her gift.

Josh stood too. "You're my little cheerleader," he said to Nadia. Then his gaze met Harley's, blindingly intense and brilliantly blue. "You always seem to know how to put a smile on her face."

"Cuz she's Miss Harley." Nadia acted like that explained everything. "She's special."

"I know." He nodded, making no attempt to stop staring at her.

The longer he stared, the harder she found it to breathe. With the setting sun at his back, there was no missing out on just how big and brawny and beautiful Josh McBride was. The tingles set in, her insides melted, and her heart was thumping like a caged rabbit's. Not that she minded. He wasn't just staring at her while wearing that blank, unreadable expression. No, he was smiling at her. A real smile. The sort of smile that made every single cell in her body sit up and take notice of him.

"You mean a lot to us, Harley," Josh said, clearing his throat.

"I'm glad." She forced herself to breathe. He'd said us. She heard it. *Us.* As much as she'd like to stand here and discuss what exactly he meant, she knew this was neither the time, nor the place.

"Harls," Grant Maxwell called out. "Hey, Harley."

"You should go find seats," Josh said, his smiling coming to an abrupt end.

"I'll cheer loud, Daddy," Nadia promised, reaching up to take Harley's hand.

"I know you will." He winked at his daughter. "You and

Harley have fun."

"We will." Harley wiggled Nadia's arm.

"Harley?" Grant was slightly out of breath. "Hey."

"Hi." Harley smiled up at him. "Where's your date?"

"I chickened out." Grant shook his head, then smiled Josh's way. "Coach McBride. Looking forward to see you boys play."

"I wanted to thank you and your father for offering to sponsor new helmets for the team. They're a hard-working group of young men. I know they'll appreciate your support." He shook Grant's hand.

"I was a Wild Cat once myself." Grant chuckled. "A long, long time ago. Glad to help out the home team."

Harley didn't miss Josh's back-and-forth look. Or Grant's back-and-forth look. Or the way the two of them sort of sized each other up.

"I hear we're in competition for Harley, here?" Grant asked, laughing.

Josh's laugh was startled. "I hear the same thing."

"What?" Harley squeaked. "What are the two of you talking about?" And why was this funny? She was mortified.

"To be your boyfriend," Nadia said. "Can we get popcorn?"

Harley was momentarily speechless. "My...boyfriend?"

"I said it should be Daddy," Nadia added. "But—"

"Okay. Popcorn. We're going." Harley cut Nadia off, shaking her head. It was bad enough that she'd humiliated herself with Josh in the parking lot of Main Street Café. She wasn't going to relive it here, on the sidelines of the stadium. "Let's go." She didn't stop to look back—she was too busy concentrating on putting one foot in front of the other.

"It jingles," Nadia said, skipping along at her side and wiggling the ribbons and bells.

By the time they'd found a seat, Harley's heart rate had returned to a somewhat regular rhythm. Not that it stopped her from developing a long list of questions about what had just happened. What was Viola North up to? What had she said? To Josh? To Grant? But more importantly, to Josh…

Still, both men seemed to find the whole thing hilarious—as if the idea of the two of them being interested in her was ridiculous. True or not, it stung.

"You okay, Miss Harley?" Nadia asked.

"I'm wonderful." Harley forced a smile. "How's the popcorn?"

Katie found them and, before long, the two girls were lost in their own conversation. Watching the two of them together brought a genuine smile to Harley's face. This was what she and Josh had wanted. This was good.

When Grant joined them, she scooched over to make him room. "That was some rapid retreat, Welsh."

She glared his way.

"What?" His dark brows rose.

She ignored him.

"Nadia?" Grant reached around her. "I'm Grant."

Nadia nodded. "I know. You can't marry Miss Harley though."

Harley closed her eyes and shook her head. "I'm not marrying anybody, Nadia."

"Definitely not me." Grant was trying very hard not to laugh. "Harley is one of my best friends."

"That's okay." Nadia smiled at him. "Friends are good."

"Yup," Katie agreed, taking more popcorn. "Want some? I'm Katie."

"Yes, please. Thank you, Katie." Grant took a handful of popcorn and chuckled.

Maybe it was his chuckling or the fact that he and Josh had acted like this was all some big joke but, whatever the reason, her pride had been dinged. It was the wrong thing to say and she knew it, but she asked anyway, "Why is this so funny?"

Grant turned to face her. "Come on, Harley, this is funny."

"Which part? That my single status is so perplexing that even a five-year-old knows who my potential dating candidates are? Or that you and Josh would both be interested in me?" An unexpected knot rose up in her throat. She turned her attention to spreading the fleece throw she'd brought over Nadia and Katie's legs.

"Look, Miss Harley. Daddy's waving," Nadia said.

She didn't want to look. "You two wave back."

Nadia and Katie waved and waved.

"I didn't mean to hurt your feelings," Grant whispered. "You know me."

She lied, "You didn't hurt my feelings." That's why she sounded like she was going to cry.

"Harley?" Grant took her hand. "I am sorry. You know if I didn't already love you so much as my friend, I'd totally fight Coach McBride for you."

She sighed. "Grant."

"No, I mean it. Of course, he would totally win. I'd probably end up in the hospital, in fact. But I'd still have tried."

She glanced his way, smiling. "You're a dork."

"Have you seen the man's arms?" He shook his head.

Yes. She had definitely seen them. *Redwood-tree arms.* Big and muscled and strong. And warm. Being wrapped up in those arms had been warm.

"But you're right. I am a dork. That's why we're friends." He wrapped his arm around her shoulders. "Besides, I get the feeling—if I was on a quest to win your heart—I'm already too late."

"Quest to win my heart?" She shook her head. "Wow. Just wow."

He shrugged. "Says the woman who is intentionally dodging my meaning."

The whistle blew and Harley took great pains to make sure that was the end of their conversation. She didn't want to talk about Josh or the fact that he had most definitely already won her heart—and he had zero interest in it. No, she wanted to scream and clap and yell and act like there was nothing more important than the Wild Cat homecoming game in progress.

And that's exactly what she did, especially when a touchdown had her, Katie, and Nadia on their feet—jumping and screaming and making all sorts of ridiculous noise. And just about the time she's scooped Nadia up for a hug, she happened to glance toward the sideline, the team, and Josh.

He was clapping, patting his players on the back, and nodding at Bernie. As he reached for the clipboard he'd set on the bench, those massive arms stretching forward, his blue eyes swiveled her way. Right before she could tear her gaze from his, he smiled. It was one of his bone-melting, stomach-flip-inducing smiles, too. There was no ignoring it—no stopping the surge of heat in the pit of her belly. Or the love in her heart.

TOWN SQUARE PARK was lined with tents, booths, food trucks, and several carnival-like rides. He promised the kids they'd have plenty of time to explore—but first things first. Josh was glad he'd skipped breakfast. He wasn't sure whose idea it was to start the morning off with a pie-eating competition but that's exactly what he was going to do.

"It's almost time, Dad." Tucker was so excited. "You can

do this." He slid the strap of Josh's duffel bag onto his shoulder.

"Where's Miss Harley?" Nadia asked, holding on to his hand.

"She's probably already there." He squeezed her hand. "We'll find her."

"Okay." Tiny bells jingled with every step Nadia took. She was wearing her mum again. She didn't care that it was no longer homecoming. To her, it was a beautiful Miss-Harley-made present meant to be worn.

After the game, he'd hoped he'd have a minute or two with Harley. But Grant Maxwell was practically glued to her side so he'd wound up saying a quick good night before packing the kids into the Jeep.

When baths were done and he was tucking Nadia into bed, she was still chattering away about Harley's gift. He'd never have figured out the meaning behind each symbol if Nadia hadn't told him. Harley had put a lot of time and thought into this—it was who she was. Nadia had wanted to sleep in her mum but he'd convinced her she might accidentally tear it, or she might lose one of the charms she treasured. As a compromise, he'd pinned it to the lampshade of her bedside lamp.

Now, bells jingling, they made their way to the table set up in front of the gazebo.

"Signing up, Coach?" Bev Washington asked, sitting at the table to supervise sign-ups.

He was a competitive person—it was sort of a job requirement when you were a coach. But he never should have let Noah's dig, teasing or not, goad him into taking the bait. Pie eating was not a *sport* he exceled in.

"And he's going to win." Tucker nodded.

"I just bet he will," Mrs. Washington said. "And you've got your own cheering section."

"I do. So I'll have to win, won't I?" Josh laughed.

"In your dreams," Noah Contreras said, clapping a hand on Josh's shoulder. "I'm warning you, I'm on a lucky streak. But I welcome the competition."

"Lucky streak?" Josh asked. "Does that mean you have good news to share?"

"I asked and she said yes." Noah's smile said everything.

"Congratulations, Noah. I'm happy for you." Josh chuckled and shook the man's hand. "But, as far as the pie contest goes? You asked for it." But then, all he saw was Harley. Her hair was down, falling around her shoulders in soft curls. Her turtleneck sweater was the same warm topaz as her eyes. *Eyes that were easy to get lost in.* He cleared his throat.

"Good morning." Harley barely spared him a passing glance before smiling at his children. "How is everyone today?"

"Daddy is going to eat all the pie." Nadia shrugged. "I just want one piece."

"How about, after your daddy eats all the pie, we go win

you something yummy at the cakewalk? Maybe a cupcake or an apple dumpling." Harley waited for Nadia's enthusiastic nod. "Good. Now let's go see Noah and your daddy get covered in pie."

"You got this, Dad." Tucker gave him a thumbs-up.

Josh laughed. "I wish I had your confidence."

"Don't let looks deceive you. Noah has two hollow legs. He can eat." Autumn caught Noah's hand in hers, beaming up at him. A telltale sparkle caught the sun.

"Nice ring," Josh said. "Congratulations, really, to both of you."

"Thank you, Josh. I'm pretty ridiculously happy. Even if I don't have the right socks for this." Autumn rested her head against Noah's shoulder.

Josh paused, confused.

"Autumn has a pair of knee socks for every occasion," Harley explained. "It's a thing with her."

"Oh." Josh wasn't sure what the correct response was for that. "Sure."

Harley laughed.

So did Autumn. "All thanks aside, Coach McBride, I don't want you to be too devastated *when* my fiancé beats you."

"I appreciate the heads-up." Josh took his seat and winked at Nadia.

"Remember, this isn't about confidence. This is about hunger." Harley sat in one of the metal folding chairs in the front row, across from him, and pulled Nadia into her lap. "You just need to be really, really, *really* hungry."

"Lots of reallys," Nadia said.

"Yep." Harley winked.

There was something about sitting behind a row of banquet tables wearing a drop cloth around his neck that struck him as hysterical. Once he started laughing, Tucker and Nadia were laughing too. Then Harley.

"You're going to choke," Harley warned.

"No more laughing." But Nadia was still grinning.

He shook his head, giving Noah and the other competitors a once-over before shooting Harley a 'why-am-I-doing-this?' look.

Harley shrugged. "I don't know what you were thinking. But, yes, you do look like a giant baby." Harley giggled, her tawny eyes fixed on his face. "A giant, muscular baby." She shook her head. "Okay, you look nothing like a baby."

"Just giant and muscular?" Autumn asked, sitting by her sister.

"Well…look at him!" Harley's gaze wandered from his face.

Autumn just chuckled and shook her head…

"I'm feeling kind of judged right now." But at the moment, he didn't mind. The slow burn of awareness seemed to follow the path of Harley's gaze. He'd managed to stop himself from getting caught up in the idea of kissing Harley Welsh. But right now, with her lips slightly parted, her

cheeks flushing, and her gaze lingering on his upper arm…
He was thinking about kissing her all right.

Then the pies arrived. The more they put in front of
him, the harder it was to keep a straight face. Tucker, Nadia,
and Harley wore the same expression—their eyes increasingly
owl-like with each additional pie.

There was no competition.

"I told you." Autumn shook her head. "Noah has hollow
legs. It's the only explanation."

"I'm sorry you didn't win, Daddy. You okay?" Nadia
asked, using the corner of his drop cloth to wipe his face.
"You're sticky."

"I am." He looked down at the front of the T-shirt he'd
worn. "A mess."

"You did *dive* into pie," Harley said.

"Good thing I'm headed for the dunking booth." Josh
stood, took the duffel bag from Tucker, and headed across
the field—the others trailing after him.

"Dunking booth?" Noah grinned. "Your team know
about this?"

"Pretty sure they do." They were probably already lined
up and waiting.

"I won't get in trouble for trying to dunk you, will I?"
Tucker asked, running ahead.

"No." He laughed.

"Let's go." Tucker grabbed Nadia's hand, pulling her
toward the waiting dunking booth. Noah trotted after them.

"I'll be right there." Josh grinned, pausing long enough to tug his pie-covered T-shirt up and over his head. He used the back to finish mopping the residual stickiness clinging to his chin. "Did I get it?" he asked.

Harley and Autumn turned at the same time.

Autumn blinked, glanced at her sister, mumbled something and followed Noah and the kids.

Harley, on the other hand, didn't move. He'd never seen that expression before—he didn't know what to make of it, but it didn't look good.

"Bad?" he asked, wiping his face again. "Do you mind?" He held the shirt out.

Harley took the shirt but didn't move. She was staring at his chest. Staring at him.

"Harley?" He frowned, finding no sign of pie anywhere he could see.

"Fine," she whispered. "Put a shirt on." But she kept staring. "Here." She pressed his pie-covered shirt back into his hands and drew in a raspy, wavering breath. She made an odd sound, so soft he had to lean forward to hear it.

"What?" he asked, stepping forward. Once she finally looked up at him, he regretted it. Not that he didn't like what he saw—but that there was no way he could do anything about it. This time, there was no denying they both felt the current pulling them together—no fighting it. He didn't want to. He wanted to give in to the ache she stirred, the yearning to hold her close. How was he supposed to walk away from her now? Now, when there was absolutely no doubt that Harley Welsh might just want him to kiss her, too. "Harley." Her name was broken and gruff. "We need to talk."

She nodded.

"But you have to stop looking at me like that or I will kiss you."

"You will?" she whispered.

It was his turn to nod.

"You should put a shirt on." She blinked, stepped back, and hurried toward the dunking booth—and his waiting football team.

Chapter Eleven

"Good?" Harley asked, taking a bite out of her caramel apple. "What would you like to do next?"

Nadia asked, "Can we do the cakewalk again?"

"What about getting your face painted first? Look, there's Katie." Harley pointed. This booth was the high school cheerleaders' fundraiser.

Nadia squealed. "Let's go."

Harley was fine with anything that kept her busy—preferably away from Josh McBride. She'd never acted that way, ever. But now…people had seen them. Autumn, Noah, the football team and who knew who else.

Autumn had tried to reassure her that there'd been nothing to see but that wasn't possible. She'd been staring, mesmerized more like it. For a good solid five minutes, she hadn't been sure she'd be able to resist the urge to reach for Josh. He'd been… He was… Her heart rate immediately picked up. He had an incredible chest. Incredible. Muscular. Gorgeous. And, most distractingly, naked. All she could think about was touching him.

And then he'd said he wanted to kiss her?

"Miss Harley." Nadia tugged on her hand. "Can I get a paw print on my cheek?"

Harley saw that Katie had a paw print on her cheek. "Yes." Harley smiled. "But you can pick from any of the designs on that poster."

"There you are." Autumn jumped in line with them. "Every time I turn around, you two are doing something else."

Harley shrugged. "I just want to make sure Nadia gets to do everything she wants to."

Autumn nodded—but she obviously wasn't buying it.

"Where is your handsome fiancé?" Harley smiled.

"He and Tucker and Josh are doing some relay race." She hooked arms with Harley, her smile dreamy. "I'm engaged."

"You're engaged." Harley hugged her. "I approve of your pick, by the way. He's a good guy."

"I'm glad to hear it. I'd hate to call it off." Autumn grinned. "You fully recovered from your naked-chest incident?"

Harley sighed. "Autumn..."

"I don't blame you. That is some chest." Autumn hugged her arm.

Harley looked at her sister. "Yes. It is."

"If it makes you feel any better, he looked just as ready to tackle you as you were to tackle him," Autumn said.

"Really?" She frowned.

"Yes." Autumn nodded again. "He so wanted to—"

"No, really as in that's supposed to make me feel better?" She shook her head. Actually, it did. But it didn't do a thing to tone down her embarrassment. "He wants to talk."

"I think that is one of the things he wants to do." Autumn grinned and raised her eyebrows.

"Autumn," Harley growled, glancing Nadia's way. Nadia was too busy talking with Katie to hear anything she and Autumn were talking about.

"After what I saw today, you can't convince me otherwise."

After face painting, they walked through the booths and tents devoted to carnival games. From tossing rings at milk bottles, darts and balloons, spraying water guns to fill up buckets, or bowling—they managed to win a squeaky penguin, two blinky necklaces, and one inflatable crown. Nadia wore them all, the penguin tucked under her arm.

"Funnel cake." Autumn tugged her toward the vendor. "We can't call it a night without funnel cake."

"Smells yummy." Nadia sniffed the air.

"It tastes even better." Harley offered Nadia a sip from her water bottle.

"Thank you." Nadia handed it back, then lit up, waving her arms and yelling, "Daddy! Over here."

Harley managed not to run or react, though she did avoid eye contact with Josh. It helped that he was wearing a shirt now, too.

"Funnel cake?" Josh scooped up Nadia. "What's all this?"

"Miss Harley won it for me." Nadia grinned.

"She has unbelievable aim," Autumn jumped in. "Growing up, if I saw something in one of the booths that I wanted, Harley would get it for me."

Noah and Tucker came running up, a massive bear over Tucker's shoulder.

"Tucker's pretty good, too," Josh said, ruffling his son's hair.

"Daddy." Nadia patted Josh's chest. "My tummy hurts real bad."

"It does?" Josh frowned.

"Uh-huh." Nadia nodded. "Can we go home now?"

"I'm sorry." Harley ran a hand along Nadia's back. "I didn't know you were feeling bad, sweetie."

Nadia rested her head on Josh's shoulder, dislodging her inflatable crown.

"I'll have to head home anyway." Josh glanced at his watch. "I'm supposed to chaperone the homecoming dance tonight."

"No, Daddy." Nadia's lower lip wobbled. "Please."

"I have to, sweetie." Josh held her close. "Mrs. Reed will come over and read to you."

"I want Harley," Nadia said, crying softly. "Please, Miss Harley."

"Of course." Harley felt terrible. It was probably her fault that Nadia's stomach was upset. She'd been in such a frenzy to keep away from Josh that she'd bounced from booth to booth, eating treats along the way. The only non-sweet thing she could remember Nadia eating were some fried chicken strips. Not exactly a healthy choice.

It didn't take long for Nadia's tears to bring Josh around to her way of thinking. Before long, Harley was following the McBride Jeep to their house and helping Tucker carry in all the prizes and trinkets they'd collected that day.

"That was awesome," Tucker said, half-carrying, half-dragging the massive teddy bear upstairs. "Tomorrow is the hay ride and the corn maze?"

She nodded. "You take a hay ride from Town Square Park all the way out to Krieger Farms. There's a corn maze and some more games and a dance for anyone who wants to stick around. It should be warm enough this year, too."

"Cool." Tucker disappeared at the top of the stairs, the sound of running water assuring her he was following his father's instructions to take a shower before dinner.

A quick inventory revealed all the ingredients she'd need to make a soothing chicken soup, just the thing for Nadia's tummy. As soon as the soup was simmering, she whipped up a quick batch of homemade biscuits.

"What's that?" Nadia asked, wearing her long-sleeve flannel nightgown and looking utterly adorable.

"Soup. Want to see?" she asked, lifting Nadia up to peer inside the pot. "Look good? I'm hoping it will help your tummy."

Nadia rested her head on her shoulder. "Miss Harley?"

"Yes, sweetie." She carried her to the couch and sat, holding Nadia close.

"I love you, Miss Harley." Nadia's hand reached up, smoothing the long curls into place.

Harley pressed a kiss to the top of her head, her heart so full. Three little words that led to pure happiness. "I love you too."

"I thought so," Nadia said, smiling up at her.

"You're smart." Harley laughed, tapping the tip of Nadia's nose. "Are you comfortable? I can get you some water or a blanket before I finish dinner." Luckily, the living, dining, and kitchen were all one large shared space so she wouldn't have to worry about not hearing or seeing Nadia if the little girl needed something.

Nadia lay back on the couch, then curled onto her side. "No, thank you."

Harley stood, smoothed Nadia's still-damp hair from her shoulder and headed back into the kitchen...where Josh was waiting. And this Josh, in slacks and a starched button-down shirt, was almost as distractingly handsome as shirtless Josh.

"You sure you'll be okay?" he asked, buttoning his cuff.

"Of course." She stirred the soup and took a peek at the biscuits in the oven.

"I was going to warm up some leftovers." He lifted the lid, shook his head, and turned her way.

"Soup will help her stomach." Despite the best of intentions, she was looking straight into those incredible blue eyes. The kitchen grew inordinately warm. The urge to touch him or hold him or *something* was so strong, she gripped the edge of the marble countertop behind her to steady herself. "But I have your number, in case we need—"

Josh took two long steps and before she knew what was happening, she was wrapped up in his arms. He sighed. Not an impatient sigh. More like…relief. *If only that were true.* Because, for her, being in his arms—finally—was a relief. She hadn't realized just how much she'd needed this until now. She closed her eyes, losing herself in Josh—just for a minute. Resting against his chest, she could hear the rapid-fire beat of his heart. Through the starched cotton of his shirt, she could breathe in his earthy-mint aftershave. Against her back, his palm pressed her close—his fingers splayed wide.

Her arms slid around his waist, holding on.

"Dad?" Tucker called from upstairs. "Dad?"

Josh exhaled, his breath brushing against her temple before his hold loosened on her. "I'm glad you're here." He stared down at her, his gaze slowly sweeping over her face.

"Me too." She sounded far more breathless than he was.

"Dad?" Tucker called again.

She smiled. "I think Tucker needs you."

He nodded.

The instant he let her go, she missed his touch. She tried to play it off, to act like the soup needed her immediate attention. But, really, she was reeling from what was happening. Yes, they were attracted to each other. That was no longer up for debate. But did that mean he loved her? Did that mean he'd changed his mind about a future for them?

There was no denying that she loved Josh with her whole heart. For Harley, there was nothing she wanted more than a future with Josh and the family she already considered hers.

JOSH HAD NOTHING but fond memories of high school. He'd liked school, loved playing sports, and hanging out with his friends. But tonight, Crossvine Creek High School was the last place he wanted to be.

Not with Harley waiting at home. Not when he had so much he wanted to say. Beginning with 'I'm an idiot' and ending with 'I love you and I hope you'll give us a chance.' He'd run through a dozen or more scenarios in his mind— doing absolutely nothing to ease the anticipation and worry that had his stomach and lungs and heart twisted up.

He checked his phone. No texts. Hopefully Nadia's stomach was better.

No matter what the large clock on the gym wall said, the two-hour dance seemed to stretch into four hours—or longer. After an hour or so, he'd checked his phone again, to make sure he hadn't missed anything from Harley. He hadn't.

Do something. Josh served punch, collected fallen bits of

crepe paper streamers, popped balloons, and separated those couples that were a little too close on the dance floor. If there was something he could do to occupy himself, he did it.

"Looks like you didn't freeze to death in the dunking booth," Bernie said, popping one of the cookies from the snack tray into his mouth. "From where I was standing, it looked like every player on the team tried to knock you into the water."

"And almost every one of them succeeded." He grinned. "I was a jerk this last week—I figure I deserved it."

"I don't know about that." Bernie shrugged, but he was chuckling. "You seem better now. Have anything to do with what the boys are talking about?" There was laughter in his voice. "I hear some of them made a bet on whether or not you were going to start dating Harley Welsh."

Josh just about choked on his punch. He shouldn't be surprised. They'd been out in the open for the whole town to see. He *had* been surprised Viola North or Bev Washington hadn't appeared out of nowhere—megaphones and carrier pigeons at the ready. "That sounds like a risky bet."

"Well, there's still time," Bernie said, but let it drop. He spent the next hour working through the upcoming games and their chances at progressing to state.

Listening to Bernie helped. For a while, football took center stage in Josh's mind. But Bernie went in hunt of another cookie and left Josh long enough for his thoughts to drift back to Harley.

By ten thirty, Josh was pacing.

At eleven, he broke down tables and took out the trash.

He was pulling into this driveway by eleven fifteen.

From the street, he could only make out a single down-stairs lamp burning. Hopefully Nadia was sound asleep and she hadn't gotten sick. Harley hadn't called but, knowing Harley, she'd have handled things without his help.

He opened the door, aware of every creak and shift in the wood floor beneath his feet. He slipped off his shoes and moved carefully down the hall and into the living room, doing his best not to make any sound.

Harley was on the sectional couch—half on the couch and half on the ottoman. Nadia lay on top of her, her little head against Harley's shoulder and her arm draped across her chest. On the opposite side of the sectional was Tucker, curled into a ball beneath his favorite blanket. A tower of story books rested on the floor next to Harley.

As much as he didn't want to wake them, it was late and Harley needed to get home. There were things the two of them needed to discuss before his neighbor, Bev Washington, informed the town that Harley had spent the night there—no matter how tempting that sounded. Watching Harley sleep, her arms wrapped around Nadia, he figured the talk could wait one more day—until they were both rested and clearheaded.

Chances were he wouldn't get much sleep, but…

"Tucker." He bent, smoothing his son's thick hair from

his face. "Tucker."

Tucker's eyes opened, but just barely.

Josh smiled. "Tucker?"

Tucker sat up, blinking and grabbing for his blanket. "I'm up."

"Shh," Josh chuckled. "Can you make it to your room?"

Tucker stood, yawned, and—dragging his blanket behind him—headed up the stairs. Seconds later, he heard the sound of a door shutting.

Harley and Nadia made quite a picture. There was no way Harley was comfortable, not with Nadia's elbow and knees poking her from odd angles. But her breathing was deep, so it must not have bothered her too much.

He knelt by the couch. "Harley?" he whispered.

Her eyes fluttered open. "Hi." She held Nadia close, slowly sitting up. "I'd meant to get them to bed… But she's been sick twice and I didn't feel right about leaving her alone."

"You should have called me."

"We were fine." Harley yawned.

"You need sleep, too. It was a long day." He nodded. "I'll take her upstairs."

She leaned forward, carefully easing Nadia into his arms.

"Daddy?" Nadia stirred. "Miss Harley?" She held her hand out.

Harley stood. "I'm here." She took Nadia's hand.

"Night." Nadia yawned. "I love you."

"I love you, too." Harley held on to his arm, stood on tiptoe, and pressed a kiss to Nadia's cheek. "Sweet dreams."

There was a fragile intimacy to it all. The quiet darkness. The weight of his daughter in his arms. The brush of Harley's hair against his arm. All of it felt...right. As if they were a family. He only wished he could see Harley's expression.

"Can you wait?" he asked. "I know it's late—"

"I'll wait." Her hand squeezed his arm.

Nadia was sound asleep by the time he had the blankets tucked around her. Josh checked on Tucker, turned on the hall night-light, and headed back downstairs.

The kitchen light was on and Harley was doing dishes.

Of course. "Harley." He gripped her shoulders and turned her to face him, taking the soap-covered dish from her hands. "I didn't ask you to stay to clean up." He released her and stepped back—he needed the space.

She nodded. It was the same. Just like the park. The two of them enclosed in sort of a current-charged bubble, all their emotions right beneath the delicate surface—trying to break through. The look on her face almost wiped the questions he had from his brain. Almost.

"You and Grant Maxwell?" He cleared his throat.

She frowned, wiping her hands on a kitchen towel. "What about him?"

"Are you two dating?" He shoved his hands into his pockets, to stop himself from reaching for her.

"No. Grant is a dear friend. That's all." She leaned back

against the kitchen counter. "Just because Viola North says something, that doesn't make it true, Josh."

He watched her fingers tighten on the kitchen counter-top, watched the unsteady rise and fall of her sweater as she breathed. She was so beautiful—so soft. He didn't know why he'd put up such a fight before. Then again, she'd been just as resistant as he was.

"When we talked before…"

She blew out a slow breath and stared at the floor.

"Harley, I feel like something has changed between us." He paused, but she didn't look up. "I'm not good at reading people. Relationships aren't my strong point."

"We have that in common." But she still wouldn't look at him.

"This would be a lot easier if you'd look at me." He stepped forward, hesitated, then tilted her chin up.

She blinked, her eyes almost topaz beneath the fluorescent kitchen lights.

Beautiful. "I…my family has lost so much." He shook his head and gave up, stepping closer, his hand cradling the curve of her cheek.

"I know. *Too* much." Her hand covered his. "My heart truly aches for you all."

He believed her. She'd lost people too. She'd been hurt. But, if she'd give him a chance, they both had a shot at happiness here. Surely, she felt this?

He bent forward, then paused, his heart at odds with his

head. There were things to say. But when she reached out, when her fingers trailed along his jaw, his heart won.

His lips met hers, tentative at first. Light, feather-like kisses. His arm found its way around her waist, pulling her more firmly against him. The feel of her arching into him—of her fingers pressing into the back of his neck—opened the floodgates.

He'd never intended to kiss her like this. To get so caught up that all that mattered was the next kiss, the next touch, the mix of her breath with his. Hearing the hitch in her breathing nearly brought him to his knees.

She had no idea what she did to him. More importantly, she had no idea what she meant to him. "Harley." He tore his lips from hers. "Wait."

She was breathing hard, her hands gripping his shirt-front. By the time her hold had loosened and she'd smoothed the creases from his shirt, he wanted to kiss her all over again.

His thoughtfully constructed speech went out the window. Instead, he blurted out, "You said you didn't want us to happen." He swallowed.

She blinked, her forehead creasing. "I did." She blew out a deep breath. "After you said we *couldn't* happen—that you had nothing more to give." She stepped back. She looked…hurt.

He *had* said that. *Idiot.* "Because I was scared."

She blinked, once, then again—her topaz eyes searching

his. "Of?"

"Of the kids getting hurt." He shook his head. "No, I didn't want to be hurt. With you... It's a real fear."

There was a thump from upstairs, followed by crying.

"Nadia?" Harley headed to the stairs.

"Daddy," Nadia was wailing.

Josh ran up the stairs to Nadia's room. "I'm here."

"I'm going to throw up," Nadia was crying. "My tummy."

"It's okay." He scooped her up and headed for the bathroom, rubbing her back the whole way. He placed a folded towel on the floor, set Nadia on it, and sat right behind her—supporting her. "It's okay."

"I'm okay now," Nadia said, her red-rimmed eyes peering up at him.

"Let's give it a minute," he soothed. Her stomach was making all sorts of not-so-normal sounds. They were right where they needed to be.

"Okay, Daddy." She leaned against him.

Harley appeared in the doorway seconds later, a towel and clean nightgown in her arms. "In case." She set them on the counter. "What can I do?"

He shook his head. "Go home. Get some sleep." He opened his mouth, then stopped. He was *not* going to declare his love to her now. He might not be a romantic, but even he knew better.

"Are you sure?" She wasn't looking at him, she was worrying over Nadia. Because she loved his daughter.

"I'm sure." He kept rubbing Nadia's back, smiling when his daughter curled against his chest. "The worst might be over."

The indecision on her face meant more than she'd ever know. "I hate leaving you like this."

"I know." Something in his voice drew her gaze. "This isn't exactly the way I'd pictured the evening ending. Thank you, for tonight."

She nodded, her features softening. "Okay. I'll see you tomorrow... Maybe." And she was gone.

Nadia ended up needing the clean nightgown. When she finally fell asleep, it was fitful so Josh squeezed into the single bed beside her. But his eyes still popped open at five thirty the next morning, so climbing over his daughter—without waking her—wasn't easy.

He was scooping coffee into the coffee maker when he saw a yellow sticky note stuck to the side of the machine. He pulled it off and read it.

I was scared too. – Harley

He smiled, folded the sticky note, and tucked it into the pocket of his jeans. He wasn't scared anymore. No. When it came to his feelings for Harley, there was a certainty he didn't question. This, she, was it. For the first time in a long time, he was filled with hope.

Chapter Twelve

HARLEY WAS NERVOUS. Good nervous. Excited nervous. And absolutely terrified nervous. From the minute she'd left Josh's house last night, to the minute she'd rolled out of bed this morning, she'd been preparing herself for either possible outcome.

She hoped he'd been on the verge of telling her exactly what she wanted to hear. That he loved her and…well, that was enough. But there was still a chance it could go the other way. He'd lost so much, he might never be in a place to try again. The attraction part was irrefutable, but the love and family and happy ending part was far from settled.

"You're awful quiet this morning." Autumn poured coffee into their travel mugs. "What's on your mind?"

Harley took the cup her sister offered. "Josh."

Autumn set her cup on the counter. "Spill."

And Harley did. All of it. What happened, what she hoped would happen, what she feared might happen. All the little aches and tingles, the not so little love and want. She needed to talk through it—to make sense of it. To, hopefully, get a better idea of how things were going to work out.

"Wow," Autumn said, studying her sister. "Just, wow."

Harley nodded. "Did you know? With Noah? I mean, should I know if he loves me? Or is this whole walking a tightrope between bliss and despair thing like…normal?"

That's when she realized her father, Noah, and Cynthia were standing in the kitchen doorway.

"It's normal." Noah headed to the coffee machine like this was any old conversation. "Until she said she loved me, I was ready to throw up. Even more so when I proposed."

"You might as well weigh in, too," Harley said to her dad and Cynthia, as she slumped into a chair at the kitchen table, her cheeks hot. "There's no pretending you didn't just hear all of *that*."

"Well said." Cynthia patted her shoulder. "If that boy doesn't love you, good riddance, I say."

Harley smiled up at her father's girlfriend.

Her father remained silent. He poured himself a cup of coffee and sat in the chair across from her before saying, "Sounds like you need to tell him how you feel."

"Just like that?" she asked.

Noah and her father nodded.

"Don't beat around the bush." Noah shook his head.

"No point wasting time," her father added. "If he's the one, make sure he knows it. Get on with building the life, together, that you want."

Harley stood and went around the table, hugging her father. "And if he doesn't want what I want?"

Her father looked up at her. "Then you tried. You took a chance at happiness. That's all I want for both of you. Happiness."

Harley spent an hour picking out what to wear. She didn't know why. Hay rides and corn-row mazes weren't exactly dress-up events. But declaring her love was. So, piece by piece, she threw sweaters and skirts onto her bed.

"Here." Autumn picked a caramel long sleeve T-shirt, black jeans, and a long red knit scarf. "Your lace-up boots, too. You can't wear heels in a corn maze."

Harley dressed, then waited for Autumn and Noah to leash Cobie and Baxter, and they all walked to Town Square Park.

Her phone pinged. "It's a text from Josh. He said the kids will be coming with Mrs. Reed. Something came up at school and he'll meet us out at Krieger Farms later."

It wasn't exactly the news she was hoping to hear. While walking right up to Josh and telling him she loved him would do a number on her nerves, both Noah and her father seemed to think that was the way to go.

"I'm sorry." Autumn took her hand. "The waiting part is the worst of it."

True. Unless he reiterated his whole 'I can't do this thing' spiel. Even though she wanted to believe that he loved her, there was that constant, nagging little voice in the back of her head that was all too pleased to repeatedly remind her that attraction didn't equate to love.

Three tractors and a flat-bed trailer piled high with hay were waiting along Main Street. It was a twenty-minute tractor drive from Town Square Park to Krieger Farms—short enough to enjoy, but long enough to appreciate the ride ending.

Harley's inner artist was awestruck by the brilliant orange, yellow, and rusty red of the park leaves beneath the morning sun. The nip in the air was just another reminder that fall was finally here.

"Miss Harley!" Nadia ran across the leaf-strewn grass, her arms outstretched.

Harley caught her. "Good morning. How is your stomach?"

"All better." Nadia hugged her.

"I'm so glad." She hugged her back, waving at Tucker and Chewie running their way.

"Hey, Miss Harley." Tucker gave her a one-armed hug. "Dad said he was sorry he couldn't be here for the ride."

"Being the new head coach in town is a big job." Harley wasn't sure what had kept him from the hay ride but at least he was meeting them later. She'd waited this long—a little longer couldn't hurt. "Chewie looks excited about it."

Chewie, Baxter, and Cobie were in full tail-wag mode, delighted to be reunited.

"They're friends." Nadia smiled, patting each dog on the head. "Hi, Miss Autumn and Mr. Noah."

Autumn giggled. "Mr. Noah."

Noah shook his head. "Morning, Nadia. Hey, Tucker. You guys ready to go?"

"How are you all, this morning?" Mrs. Reed asked, eyeing the dogs. "My goodness, what a lively crew."

"Mrs. Reed, I can take the children if you'd like. I'm sure Josh wouldn't mind—"

"Nope." Tucker shook his head. "Dad said we need to stay with Mrs. Reed today."

Nadia burst out laughing. "Yep."

Harley looked back and forth between them.

"Now, children." Mrs. Reed steered them to the tractor, whispering as they went.

"That was weird, wasn't it?" Harley asked her sister. "Right?"

Autumn shrugged. "Maybe he felt bad, Harley, after last night. Taking care of a sick kid is sort of a lot to ask."

"I volunteered," she argued.

"Maybe Mrs. Reed needs the money," Noah volunteered.

That makes sense. At least, that made her feel better.

Jeans had been the right choice to wear today. There was nothing like climbing up a stack of hay bales to confirm that. But she wanted the kids to have the best view. Now they sat, Tucker beside her and Nadia in her lap, ready to go. After Mrs. Reed assured them she preferred riding lower, Autumn climbed up too—leaving Noah in charge of the dogs.

The roar of the tractor engine made conversation difficult, but they managed. Harley and Autumn pointed out the studio, the elementary school, the high school, and they waved at everyone they passed as they made their way out of town.

"What's that?" Tucker asked, pointing to the side of the road.

"What?" Autumn asked, leaning forward to see.

Nadia giggled. "That. See, Miss Harley?"

Harley turned. "Is that Ashley?"

"The cheerleader." Nadia giggled some more.

Ashley waved, holding up the sign.

Autumn read the sign, "Harley Welsh…"

"It's your name," Tucker said, winking at Nadia.

"It is…" Harley glanced at her sister, beyond mystified.

"I have no idea." Autumn held up both hands.

A mile down the road, two football players had another sign. "Will you…" Then another, "meet me…" This time, Bernie Ulrich was there, waving. His sign read, "in the maze?"

"Will you meet me in the maze?" Autumn sucked in a deep breath. "Is this from Josh?"

"Look, look." Nadia pointed. "One more."

This sign was tied to the side of Noah's green truck—balloons waving in the breeze. All this one said was "Coach McBride." But there was an all-glitter heart, too.

Harley's heart was in her throat, hammering so hard that even the tractor engine couldn't drown out the noise.

"Noah?" Autumn stared at her fiancé. "You know?"

Noah shrugged. "I don't know what you're talking about." But he and Mrs. Reed exchanged a wink.

Harley peered down the road, the farm still too far away.

"It's from Daddy." Nadia smiled up at her. "We made them this morning. I did the glitter heart."

"Dad tried but it was lopsided," Tucker explained.

Josh and glitter? She remembered his clove apple attempt, and him saying he wasn't artistic. But he'd tried. For her.

"It was." Nadia nodded. "And we went to the school and the team was there waiting."

"Nadia." Tucker shot her a look.

"Oops." Nadia pressed her lips together. "We're not supposed to tell you what Daddy said to them."

"So, stop talking." Tucker covered her mouth with his hand, but he was laughing.

Nadia started giggling all over again.

"Are you breathing?" Autumn asked, taking her hand.

"I think so." Was she? She wasn't sure. At the moment, she was pretty consumed with anticipation. "Has it always taken this long to get out to Krieger Farms?"

Autumn laughed, giving her hand a squeeze. "We must be taking the long way—so he had room for all his signs."

"I can't believe he did this," Harley murmured. He'd said he was scared. But this? This wasn't just facing his fears, this was putting them out there for everyone to see. As soon as she saw him, as soon as she reached him, she'd make sure he knew—when it came to her—he had nothing to fear. She loved him. He was the one. And she couldn't wait to tell him.

JOSH HEADED STRAIGHT for Viola North and her friends, clustered together beneath a large oak tree to enjoy their hot chocolate. "Good morning."

"Good morning to you, too, Coach." Bev smiled.

"Where are you precious children?" Jentina Ramos asked. "Are they in the maze?"

"They're on their way here, with Harley and Mrs. Reed." He ran a hand along the back of his neck. "I thought you should know that I am in pursuit of Miss Harley Welsh. I know you ladies have an interest in pairing up the singles in Crossvine Creek, so I thought I'd give you notice. You can take me off the list."

Seeing their shock and surprise was far more gratifying than he'd expected.

Viola North recovered first. "And Miss Harley Welsh?"

"I'll let you know in about ten minutes." The rest of his team had arrived and he was running out of time. "Enjoy your hot chocolate, ladies."

With Mr. Krieger's help, he and his players placed signs along the path—signs Harley would follow to find him. Up until now, he'd thought this was a solid plan. He'd never done something like this—never even considered it. But this was Harley. Last night had stripped away all his fear and doubt.

It was pretty straightforward. He loved her and wanted a future with her. And, he felt the need to make sure everyone—Grant Maxwell and Viola North and all—knew that. But now, he'd lined the streets with signs, recruited the football team, the cheerleading squad and Harley's sister's fiancé…there was no going back.

This could backfire and then what? "Is this a mistake?" he asked, not intending to actually voice his concern.

"Why would it be?" old man Krieger asked. "You like her well enough."

He smiled.

"She's not one of those fancy women, needing fancy things," Mr. Krieger added.

Not that Josh would mind giving her something fancy.

"She's got a good heart, too. Loves kids." Mr. Krieger looked at him, frowning. "It'd be a mistake not to go after the girl." He eyed the signs they'd almost finished placing. "Not sure about all the hubbub and nonsense, but you young people seem to like it so it might just help bring her around."

Which wasn't exactly a confidence-building thing to hear but he couldn't argue with it. Hopefully, his harebrained, over-the-top, public display would show her just how serious he was about her.

Mr. Krieger had found the perfect spot, off a long lone trail he said high school kids used for all sorts of romancing. Josh didn't ask what that meant—he was pretty sure he didn't want to know. Now he was pacing the patch of dirt, listening to the rustle of dried corn stalks and the rise and fall of voices carried on the wind.

He heard the tractor engine.

He waited.

Then, finally, he heard Tucker say, "This way." And Nadia's laugher. Some barking.

"Are you sure?" Harley asked. She sounded nervous.

Josh blew out a deep breath, slowly. It didn't help. Like her, he was nervous.

"I'm sure," Tucker said. "Bye."

"Bye, Miss Harley. Tell Daddy hi." He could hear the smile in Nadia's voice.

He smiled, too.

"Come on, kids," Mrs. Reed said. "Let's go through the maze and then we'll get some hot chocolate."

More rustling and then silence.

He rolled his neck, shook out his hands, and waited. The longer he waited, the heavier his chest felt.

And then, she was there—moving toward him.

"Hi." He smiled tentatively.

"Hi?" She blinked. "Hi?"

"Too much?" He was hard pressed not to stare. She was about the most beautiful thing he'd ever seen. This morning, especially so.

Her gaze wandered over his face. "I don't know yet."

He nodded. "I was trying to get your attention."

"You have it." She smoothed the hair from her shoulder. Her hand was shaking.

He caught her hand, holding it in both of his. "I told Viola North to take me off the list."

"You what?" She stared up at him.

"Just now. I told her I didn't need her fixing me up with anyone." He cleared his throat. "I told her I'd let her know about you when this was through."

She swallowed, hard, her fingers tightening on his. "When...*what* was through?"

All the air in his lungs disappeared. "Me." There was too much space between them. "Telling you that I love you."

One second Harley was standing in front of him, the next she was pressed against him, her face buried against his chest, her arms around his neck. "I was hoping that was what you'd say." Her hands were still shaking.

"I'm glad." His nose ran along her temple, breathing her in. "Even though I come with baggage."

"I adore your baggage." She looked up at him.

"And they love you." He ran his fingers through her hair, taking his time to study her. "I should have told you a while back."

"I didn't say anything either." She shook her head. "I thought, well, that night in the parking lot sort of shot down any hope I had for the two of us."

"Yeah, well." He chuckled. "You were pretty convincing yourself. I felt like a fool for believing you'd be interested in me." He wrapped one long curl around his finger.

"I'm interested, Coach McBride," she said in a whisper. "I love you, fiercely. In fact, I find myself constantly fighting against the need to touch you."

It was much easier to breathe then. Much easier to think. "Same."

"But, I guess, since I love you and you love me, it's okay?" Her gaze fell to his mouth.

It was an invitation he immediately accepted.

Kissing her was a full-bodied experience. There was nothing sweeter than the taste of her mouth or how eagerly she held herself against him. She gave him all she had. One kiss gave way to another, the need to keep the other close stronger with each touch.

The echo of voices on the wind was the only thing that brought him back to where they were.

"Does this mean I get to tell Nadia you're my girlfriend?" he asked, kissing her cheek.

"Am I?" she asked breathlessly.

"For now." He tilted her head back again, loving the way she looked at him. "I thought it was too soon to ask for more."

Her eyes widened.

He kissed her. "I don't want to rush things. I'm not going anywhere. Not ever." He ran his thumb along her lower lip. "I came here for a fresh start, to give my kids a fresh start. At least, that's what I thought."

She leaned into his touch. "I'm glad you did."

"But it turns out I was wrong." He shook his head. "I came here for you, Harley Welsh. Because, wherever you are, that's where I—where the kids and I—belong."

She was on her tiptoes, her arms tight around his neck as she kissed him. "Josh McBride," she whispered between kisses. "You can tell everyone I'm your girlfriend. Well, actually, I think you already have."

"Guess I'll have to come up with something even bigger when I propose," he agreed, meeting her kiss for kiss.

She grinned up at him. "Oh really?"

"You'll just have to wait and see." He cradled her face in his hands.

"Not too long." There was an earnestness that filled his heart.

He shook his head. "Not too long." He rested his forehead against hers. "I love you."

"I love you, too." She took his hand. "Now, I want to hug those kids of yours. And then I have something I need to tell Viola North."

He held her hand up, kissed her knuckles, and followed her down the path. "I'm a fan of this whole Pumpkin Patch Fall Festival now."

She stared back at him. "You are?"

"If it wasn't for that checklist of yours, none of this would have happened." He pulled her to a stop. "Viola can wait."

Want more? Check out Autumn and Noah's story in
Dog Park Sweethearts!

Join Tule Publishing's newsletter for more great reads and
weekly deals!

If you enjoyed *Pumpkin Patch Sweethearts,*
you'll love the other book in….

The Welsh Sisters series

Book 1: *Dog Park Sweethearts*

Book 2: *Pumpkin Patch Sweethearts*

More books by Sasha Summers

The Draegers of Last Stand, Texas series

Book 1: *Sweet on the Cowboy*

Book 2: *Christmas Flowers*

About the Author

Sasha Summers grew up surrounded by books. Her passions have always been storytelling, romance and travel–passions she's used to write more than 20 romance novels and novellas. Now a best-selling and award winning-author, Sasha continues to fall a little in love with each hero she writes.

From easy-on-the-eyes cowboy, sexy alpha-male werewolves, to heroes of truly mythic proportions, she believes that everyone should have their happy ending–in fiction and real life.

Sasha lives in the suburbs of the Texas Hill country with her amazing and supportive family and her beloved grumpy cat, Gerard, The Feline Overlord. She looks forward to hearing from fans and hopes you'll visit her online at sashasummers.com.

Thank you for reading

Pumpkin Patch Sweethearts

If you enjoyed this book, you can find more from all our great authors at TulePublishing.com, or from your favorite online retailer.

TULE
PUBLISHING

Made in the USA
Monee, IL
19 February 2023

28202935R00136